"I—"

"Really ought t actly *what* you want,

He reached for a   from the inside drawer of his desk and scribbled down an address. "I'm traveling to Metameikos on business tomorrow afternoon. Should you wish to join me, we leave from this airstrip at four."

She did a double take. "Sorry?"

"I'm traveling to Metameikos tomorrow," he repeated, handing her the slip of paper. "Come with me and let me spend the next two weeks showing you why our getting divorced isn't in the least bit logical. If I fail, then at the end I will sign."

Libby's mouth dropped open in shock.

Self-Made MILLIONAIRES

These men will settle for nothing less than the best!

From the lowliest slums to Millionaire's Row…

Through sheer determination and passionate belief these gorgeous men have reached the top. They never rested on their laurels, never relied on fancy qualifications or inherited cash—they've fought for every penny they have.

With names synonymous with money, power and success, these men have everything now but their brides—and they'll settle for nothing less than the best!

Self-Made Millionaires is the new miniseries from Harlequin Presents®

Available this month:

Greek Tycoon, Wayward Wife
by Sabrina Philips

Sabrina Philips

GREEK TYCOON, WAYWARD WIFE

Self-Made
MILLIONAIRES

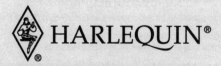

HARLEQUIN®

TORONTO • NEW YORK • LONDON
AMSTERDAM • PARIS • SYDNEY • HAMBURG
STOCKHOLM • ATHENS • TOKYO • MILAN • MADRID
PRAGUE • WARSAW • BUDAPEST • AUCKLAND

Recycling programs
for this product may
not exist in your area.

ISBN-13: 978-0-373-12924-9

GREEK TYCOON, WAYWARD WIFE

First North American Publication 2010.

Copyright © 2010 by Sabrina Philips.

This edition published by arrangement with Harlequin Books S.A.

For questions and comments about the quality of this book
please contact us at Customer_eCare@Harlequin.ca.

® and TM are trademarks of the publisher. Trademarks indicated with
® are registered in the United States Patent and Trademark Office, the
Canadian Trade Marks Office and in other countries.

www.eHarlequin.com

Printed in U.S.A.

All about the author...
Sabrina Philips

SABRINA PHILIPS first discovered Harlequin romances one Saturday afternoon in her early teens at her first job in a charity shop. Sorting through a stack of preloved books, she came across a cover featuring a glamorous heroine and a tall, dark, handsome hero. She started reading under the counter that instant—and has never looked back!

A lover of both reading and writing, Sabrina went on to study English with classical studies at Reading University. She adores all literature, but finds there's nothing *quite* like the indulgent thrill of a romance—preferably whilst lying in a hot bath with no distractions!

After graduating, Sabrina began to write in her spare time, but it wasn't until she attended a course run by Harlequin Presents® author Sharon Kendrick in a pink castle in Scotland that she realized if she wanted to be published, she had to *make* time. She wrote anywhere and everywhere and, thankfully, it all paid off, because a decade after reading her very first Harlequin novel, her first submission—*Valenti's One-Month Mistress*—was accepted for publication in 2008. She is absolutely delighted to be an author herself and to have the opportunity to create infuriatingly sexy heroes, whom she defies both her heroines and her readers to resist!

Sabrina continues to live in Guildford with her husband, who first swept her off her feet when they were both sixteen and poring over a copy of *Much Ado About Nothing* for their English A-Level. She loves traveling to exotic destinations and spending time with her family. When she isn't writing or doing one of the above, she works as deputy registrar of civil marriages, which she describes as a fantastic source of romantic inspiration and a great deal of fun.

For more information please visit www.sabrinaphilips.com.

To Phil

For planting the seed of an idea in my mind

And for keeping me sane whilst it grew

CHAPTER ONE

'I'M AFRAID, Mr Delikaris, that you are still behind Spyros in the opinion polls.'

Orion glared at the bar chart projected on the wall, and then at the pessimistic expression of his campaign manager, who sat beside him at the long, highly polished table. A nerve spasmed at his jaw in disapproval. Orion never allowed himself to contemplate failure. He expected the members of his team to think the same way. That was what he paid them for.

'We have made progress,' the man continued anxiously, sensing Orion's displeasure, 'Especially since the campaign has focussed on how much you are willing to invest in both affordable housing and the new hospital. It's just not quite as *much* progress as we had estimated.'

He clicked the button in his hand and the image on the wall changed to a far more positively weighted graph, which only served to irritate Orion further, since it proved that his team's predictions had been wholly inaccurate.

Orion pinched the bridge of his nose. 'So, despite the fact that our policies are exactly what Metameikos needs, a man who is as corrupt as his father was before him is *still* the most popular candidate?' He looked down the table at the rest of his team. 'Would anyone care to volunteer a reason why?'

A long, uneasy silence followed.

Finally a voice came from the opposite end of the table. 'Perhaps people are wary about voting for you.'

There was a collective intake of breath. Rion slowly raised his head to see who had spoken. It was Stephanos, an assistant press officer and the newest member of his team. He was also the youngest. 'Go on.'

'People see you as a billionaire bachelor who has decided overnight, or so it seems to them, that you want to be their leader.' Stephanos paused, awaiting Rion's condemnation, but it didn't come. It gave him the courage to elaborate. 'Your promises may be what people want to hear, but these results show they clearly don't trust you'll deliver them. Perhaps they think you're simply running on a whim—to try and prove that you can succeed at anything you choose—or perhaps they think that if you do get elected you'll be too tied up with your business in Athens to devote the necessary time to the role. It's not true, of course, but they don't know that. People would rather vote for the devil they know.'

Orion studied Stephanos thoughtfully. The boy had guts. He liked that. It reminded him of himself. He also understood that politics was different from business, that people voted with their hearts, not necessarily in conjunction with their heads. Orion had always understood that too, but it hadn't occurred to him that people would instinctively stick with what they had rather than take an outside chance. He would always have taken the chance.

'So, what would *you* have me do?'

The rest of the men around the table exchanged astonished looks. His campaign manager looked affronted.

Stephanos took a deep breath and continued. 'For people to trust you they need to be able to relate to you, to see that your concerns, your values, are the same as theirs—good old-fashioned Greek values.'

Orion grimaced. His values *were* good old-fashioned Greek values—always had been. 'I grew up in Metameikos,' he said gravely. What had happened there had made him who he was.

'Then convince them you still think of it as home,' Stephanos replied animatedly. 'That the house you've bought there isn't just another property, but that you plan to settle down there.'

'And how do you suggest I do that?'

'Honestly?' Stephanos paused, a note of hesitancy entering his voice for the first time, 'In my opinion, the best solution would be to return to Metameikos with a wife.'

The receptive look on Rion's face immediately vanished and his expression grew dark, 'Then I hope you have an alternative solution,' he ground out, 'because that is not an option.'

Libby stared at the huge three-dimensional Delikaris logo rotating hubristically in its own fountain, at the enormous revolving glass doors which formed the en-

trance of his state-of-the-art office, and told herself
again that this was the right thing to do. It was the same
thing she'd been telling herself ever since she'd discovered that she'd be required to cover the Greek tours for
the duration of Zoe's maternity leave.

But she'd been finding excuses not to ever since
arriving in Athens a week ago, and even now she still
had the urge to run in the opposite direction. Which was
completely and utterly ridiculous, because of *course* it
was the right thing to do. It was time they both moved
on for good. How could it be anything else when she
and Rion hadn't spoken in five years?

It was just that being back in Athens, having to pass
the city hall, the old apartment block, had brought her
memories to the surface—that was all. But that was all
they were: memories. She just felt this way because they
hadn't seen each other since back then, and she was remembering the man she'd once been in love with, when
the reality was she'd probably barely recognise him now.

If the exterior of his office was anything to go by,
he'd be much changed. And so was she. Whilst she'd
been off leading low-cost tours around the globe, with
only a guidebook and a battered rucksack on her back,
he mustn't have spent a single day out of his suit, must
have worked every hour since to achieve all this.

Was that why he'd never got his lawyers onto it,
then? Libby wondered for the umpteenth time. Had he
been so focussed on his work that the legalities had
simply slipped his mind? As she finally forced herself
to take on the revolving doors, and found herself depos-

ited in a vast, gleaming reception area, she could well believe he had.

'Can I help you?' the glossy-haired receptionist ventured, shooting a condescending glance over her tie-dyed dress and comfy leather sandals. Libby grew suddenly conscious that she was the only woman in the busy entrance hall who wasn't wearing a pair of impossibly high, pointy stilettos and a designer business suit, but she didn't let it faze her.

'I was hoping to see Orion Delikaris—'

'Have you an appointment?'

Libby knew that trying to speak to him at his office was hardly ideal, but without his address, or any means of obtaining it, she had no other alternative. 'No, but as it's lunchtime I thought—'

The receptionist tossed her head and gave a snort of laughter. 'Then you thought wrong. Mr Delikaris does not have time for a *lunch break*. He is an exceptionally busy man.'

Libby didn't need to be reminded. Didn't doubt that he'd only got busier. But surely after five years he could spare her ten minutes?

'Maybe you will be so kind as to call Mr Delikaris and let *him* decide whether he wishes to see me,' she said, with emphatic sweetness. She'd once negotiated borrowing twenty-two camels to take an entire tour group across the desert at night, when a coach hadn't turned up, so she'd be dammed if she was going to be frightened off by a woman whose deadliest weapon was immaculate grooming and an over-inflated sense of self-importance.

The woman exhaled through her teeth, wearily lifted the receiver of her phone and tapped a button with one perfectly manicured talon. 'Electra, darling, so sorry to disturb you. I have a woman here who insists that we notify Mr Delikaris that she is in Reception. Mmm. Yes, another one. She seems to think if he knows she's here he'll agree to see her.'

She turned back to Libby. 'Your name, please?'

Libby took a deep breath. 'My name is Libby Delikaris,' she replied. 'I'm his wife.'

The office was silent.

'I'm afraid there's no alternative solution as far as I can see,' Stephanos answered. 'You can continue to spend as much time in Metameikos as possible; support local businesses, attend local events and keep trying to get the Mayor on side, but I don't think anything but getting married is going to truly convince people you plan to settle down there.'

Rion grimaced. 'I repeat. Marriage is out of the question.'

Stephanos was surprised that the man who'd sworn he would stop at nothing to win this election wouldn't even consider his suggestion, but decided it would be wise to drop it. 'Oh, well, even that would have been no guarantee. Without a long-term girlfriend it might have looked a little too much like a publicity stunt—especially so close to the election.'

The intercom on the desk behind Rion suddenly burst into life.

He swooped across to it, his voice curt. 'Yes?'

'I'm very sorry to interrupt you, Mr Delikaris, but there's a woman in Reception who is demanding we inform you that she's here.'

'Who is it?'

There was a loaded pause. 'She says her name is Libby Delikaris and that…she's your wife.'

Rion didn't move—couldn't. The instantaneous flood of pleasure that ran over him was so profound it rendered him motionless.

At last she had returned. At last she deemed him worthy enough.

It was the moment he'd been waiting for—far, far too long. Not because he gave a damn about her opinion any longer, he qualified quickly. But because now, finally, he could take his revenge.

He straightened victoriously. As he did, he caught sight of his team out of the corner of his eye, and suddenly the fortuity of her timing struck him. She had chosen to come crawling back *now,* just when he needed to convince the world he was all about good old-fashioned Greek values. His eyes glittered, and his mouth curved into a sardonic smile. How convenient.

He pressed the button on the intercom and replied with perfect composure, 'Thank you. Send her up.'

Rion sensed every eye in the room widen. It was understandable; he'd never mentioned her. But then he never spoke about failed ventures or the past. Since she fell into both categories, he did his best not to even think about her. Sometimes he even succeeded.

'Apologies, gentlemen. I'm afraid we will need to continue this meeting at another time.'

The men cleared the room without another word. Only Stephanos lingered.

'You know, an alternative way of convincing people you are the settling kind *has* just this minute occurred to me,' he said wryly, looking Rion straight in the eye and walking backwards towards the door. 'Nothing melts hearts like a reunion story.'

Libby hadn't used his surname for five years; hadn't called herself his wife for just as long. If the look of shock on the receptionist's face was anything to go by, Rion hadn't mentioned her existence either. Yet it seemed his instruction to send her up immediately was proof enough that she was telling the truth, for within seconds the receptionist had become politeness personified—even explaining in detail how Libby could get to his office on the top floor via the stairs when she mentioned she'd rather not use the lift.

As she ascended the stairs, Libby ignored the doubts churning in her stomach and told herself to get a grip. What they'd had once was already lost, the emotional side of it dealt with long ago. This was just a formality, bound to be nothing more than a slightly awkward but amicable exchange between two people who were virtual strangers to one another now, she tried to convince herself. Maybe when it was over she'd even feel the complete sense of freedom she'd always been searching for but had never quite found. She clung to that thought as she arrived on the top floor, passed through a landing area, and then proceeded along a corridor to knock on a large mahogany door emblazoned with his name.

'Come in.'

Yes, in theory the emotional side *should* have been dealt with long ago, but the instant she saw him Libby knew that she had been seriously mistaken.

Of course she was well aware that Orion Delikaris was the most desirable man on the planet. She hadn't expected that to have changed. But she had expected that age and wealth would have altered him at least fractionally. Instead, to her horror, save for the fact that his suit now looked ludicrously expensive, everything was exactly as she remembered. His strong, proud jaw, his resplendent dark hair, those liquid brown eyes that had fuelled her teenage fantasies and shaped her adult ones. Which had gazed right back at her on their wedding day, their wedding night.

She blinked, blocking out the memories, blocking out the urge to run again—away from feelings she shouldn't be feeling any more. 'Hello, Rion,' she managed, somehow.

Rion ran his eyes over her, frustrated to find that the action induced the most powerful kick of arousal he'd felt in years. But he knew it was only because his body still saw her as the woman who'd rejected him, was just responding the way it did to any challenge. The second she started begging him to take her back his desire would evaporate. And yet it annoyed him that she should still get to him that way—especially when she looked so…different. The thick blond hair which had once hung in a silken curtain down her back was gone, now cut short in the kind of style he usually considered unfeminine, but which somehow made her features look even more delicate. Her petite, pale figure, which had once driven him to distraction, had also disappeared, but in its place was an even more enticing mass of toned, sensual curves tanned to a beguiling shade of golden-brown.

He gritted his teeth. Which suggested she spent her life on holiday. That would be about right: Caribbean beaches and designer shops, no doubt funded by her parents. Though somehow that image didn't seem to fit with the clothes she was dressed in. Perhaps Ashworth Motors had fallen on hard times. A perverse part of him hoped that it had. It would make telling her no—after she'd been of use to him, of course—all the sweeter.

'So tell me,' he said, unable to fathom her delay if that was the case, 'what took you so long?'

Libby was taken aback by his question, by his implacable expression that bordered on hostile, but she told herself it was understandable. She, for all the good it had done her, had at least been able to prepare herself mentally for seeing him again. He'd had no such luxury.

'I took the stairs,' she answered, looking up at the clock on the wall and noting that she'd only been five minutes. She was about to shoot out *You know I don't do lifts,* but then she remembered that he didn't know, that he'd really known so little about her, and she about him.

And they knew even less about each other now,

which was why not doing this was ludicrous. 'I apologise if this isn't a good time.'

He gave a wry smile. 'On the contrary, now is the perfect time—but that wasn't what I meant. I've been expecting you for years, Liberty.'

Libby wanted to correct him, to tell him she never let anyone call her that any more, but the revelation that he'd been expecting her, that he obviously agreed this was the right thing to be doing, was so welcome that she let it pass.

'You mean you *have* been trying to contact me? I'm sorry. I did wonder if you had, but I've been overseas almost permanently. Bank statements from three years ago are only just starting to catch up with me.'

'If I had wanted to find you I would not have failed.'

But he hadn't wanted to find her. What would have been the sense, when he'd always known she would come crawling back once he'd made it, that he would have his chance to turn the tables—make the humiliation hers instead of his? Yes, it had been far too long coming, but he wouldn't have denied himself this moment for anything—would have waited fifty years if that was what it had taken.

Libby frowned.

'I rather expected you to come back the first time my name appeared on the International Rich List. Or have you been waiting for me to reach the top ten?'

Her relief evaporated. He thought her coming here had to do with money? She stared back at him in disbelief, and in that instant she realised her initial appraisal had been wrong. He had changed. Grown harder, more cynical. Perhaps she ought to be relieved that he was the stranger to her she'd imagined after all. Instead she just felt sad. 'I don't read things like that. I never did.'

He gestured around his enormous office, to the roof-top garden adjacent and the incredible view of the Acropolis, and raised his eyebrow cynically. 'You mean you weren't aware that my circumstances have changed?'

'Of course. But that has nothing to do with why I'm here.'

Rion gave a disparaging laugh. So in many ways she was the same old Liberty Ashworth. Still intent on denying that money mattered to her. That explained her nomadic-looking clothes, at least. They were obviously just part of her plan to convince him she didn't care about material things any more.

'So, if not because of my change of circumstances, why *have* you returned?' he drawled, deciding to humour her.

Libby took a deep breath, aware that the moment had come. 'I'm here because it's been five years, and we should have sorted this out a long time ago,' she said softly, opening her bag and sliding a sheaf of papers across the table.

Rion didn't register what she was saying at first. He was too busy watching her face, the flush of colour that had risen in her cheeks at the sight of him, guessing how long she was going to keep up the act. But when he realised she was waiting for him to respond he dropped his eyes to the table—and that was when he saw it.

Libby felt a plunging sense of guilt as she watched his eyes widen in horror, guilt, and disbelief in equal measure. Surely he couldn't really be that surprised?

Petition for Divorce.

Rion stared down at the words, reeling inwardly in both shock and fury. But the shock was only momentary. It was obvious, really. Despite all he'd achieved, the millions he'd earned, he still lacked the right pedigree for the daughter of Lord and Lady Ashworth, didn't he?

'Of course,' he said bitterly.

Libby swallowed down the lump in her throat. 'Then you agree that getting this paperwork sorted is long overdue?'

He closed his eyes and drew in a deep breath, anger and agony warring in his chest. When he'd imagined the moment of her return it had never been like this.

But the second he realised that anger was starting to win out he forced his eyes open. He would *not* allow himself to feel that pain—not a second time. So she wanted a divorce? So what? He wanted one too. The only reason he hadn't had it finalised already was because he'd been waiting for the chance to savour his revenge. And who was to say this wasn't that chance anyway? Fate, he'd come to understand, worked in mysterious ways.

He looked up at her face. The flush of colour in her cheeks was bordering on crimson. She might not want to return as his wife, but it was obvious she did want his body as much as she always had, as much as he still wanted hers—whether he liked it or not. Maybe reminding her that she would never stop desiring him, however low her opinion of him remained, would be even more satisfying. Not to mention useful.

A slow smile spread across his lips. He didn't need her good opinion. He needed his wife by his side for the duration of his campaign, and he wanted her back in his bed one final time. *Then* he could discard her, exactly as she had discarded him—with a bit of luck at the exact moment he'd proved to her that her physical desire for him went deeper than any class divide.

'No, *gineka mou*,' he said deliberately, curling his tongue deliberately around the Greek for *my wife*. 'I'm sorry to disappoint you, but I don't agree.'

The hint of menace in his voice started a pulse of trepidation behind her ribcage, but she refused to accept that its presence was justified. He was just worried about getting stung financially. 'Please, have it checked out by your lawyers, if you wish. They'll confirm I'm not asking you for anything.'

'Nor would you get anything if you were,' he replied, his tone so cold that it felt as if someone had dropped an ice cube down her back, demolishing every last hope of being able to discuss this amicably as it fell.

'So enlighten me,' he continued, wondering if she actually possessed the gall to come out and say it. 'If not for money, why *do* you want to get divorced from me so badly?'

'Because it's ridiculous not to,' she justified. 'Legally we're each other's next of kin, but we don't even know each other's phone numbers any more. When I fill in a form I still have to tick the "married" box, even though I haven't seen you for half a decade. It's a lie.'

Rion looked at her intensely. 'It wasn't once.'

No, Libby thought bleakly, shocked that he'd brought emotions into it, and had managed to do so with just three small words. *It wasn't once.* A montage of images flashed through her mind: Athens under an unexpected foot of February snow, falling like nature's cold confetti. Tucking her hired wedding dress into her Wellington boots. Coercing two frozen passers-by to witness their simple ceremony in the town hall in exchange for the promise of hot chocolate. Their wedding day had been the first day in her life which *hadn't* felt like a lie.

'No,' she admitted, trying to keep her voice level, 'it wasn't once. But it is now. It's been five years.'

'Indeed it has. Five years in which you could have come asking for this, but didn't. So why now?'

She shrugged self-consciously, his words forcing her to ask herself the same question. Why *had* she waited so long? Because all this time she'd been hoping…? *No*, she'd always known they could never go back.

'I always supposed you'd get in touch about it. Then I was too busy abroad to worry, but when my job required me to come to Athens it seemed crazy not to take the opportunity to sort things out amicably, in person.'

'You think that there is an *amicable* way of divorcing your Greek husband?' He shook his head. 'Then you do not know very much about Greek men, *gineka mou*.'

'I presumed that as a Greek you were a man of

logic—able to see that there is no sense in remaining married when what was once between us has been over for half a decade.'

'If that was the case, then I would,' he breathed, and to Libby it felt as though the temperature in the room had dropped to sub-zero. 'But it's not. You still want me. I can see it. You always have, from the moment you laid eyes on me.' He took a step towards her. 'And even though you ran thousands of miles away from me, you still want me—don't you?'

Libby felt her face flush instantly crimson. 'Even if that were true, sexual attraction is no reason to stay married.' Especially sexual attraction which had been one-sided from the moment they'd said their vows, she thought wretchedly, knowing he was just trying to find ways to talk her out of it because he thought he needed to protect his bank balance.

'It's a reason that's a hell of a lot more substantial than the ones you've given me for getting divorced.'

Libby frantically searched her mind. 'That's not true. There are plenty of other reasons why getting a divorce is the most logical thing to do. I mean… maybe…maybe you'll want to marry someone else in the future.' The thought made her feel physically sick, but she ploughed on. 'Maybe I'll want to marry someone else too.' She couldn't imagine it ever being true right now, but at least it might convince him it was time they both moved on, that she had no financial motive.

'So finally we get to why you are really here,' he

breathed. 'Who is it? Let me guess. An earl perhaps? A duke?'

Libby took a sharp breath, not anticipating that he'd jump to the conclusion that she meant she was with someone *now*, but at the same time noticing the way his hand had moved back towards the divorce papers, as if he was finally starting to see sense.

'Does it matter?' she goaded.

Rion gritted his teeth in frustration, imagining some effeminate member of the English aristocracy with his hands all over her perfect body. He'd always forbidden himself to think about it in the intervening years, but he'd known her sexual betrayal was likely, for she'd been the most responsive lover he'd ever had. So responsive that at times he'd found it near impossible to show her the kind of restraint he'd thought she'd deserved. Which she never had, he thought grimly, his desire doubling at the thought of taking her with the full force of his need, proving that, even though he'd never be good enough in her eyes, no one else would ever turn her on the way he did.

'Since *I'm* your husband, I don't suppose it does matter who he is,' he said, moving his hand away from the table again.

Libby shook her head despairingly. When had he got so cold?

'But what possible advantage is there to remaining married? For the last five years I've been on the other side of the world.'

'You're not on the other side of the world any more.'

She shook her head exasperatedly, deciding to call his bluff. 'So what are you saying, that instead of signing this divorce paper you want me to back as your wife for real?'

'Yes, *gineka mou*. That's precisely what I'm saying.'

CHAPTER TWO

'You can't be serious,' she stammered.

'I'm perfectly serious.'

Libby stared at him in disbelief. How many times had she dreamed of hearing him say that? Dreamed that all this time he'd never forgotten her the way she'd never forgotten him, that now that they were both older, had had the time to find themselves, they could find one another again? More times than she wanted to admit.

It was the deeply buried part of her heart responsible for those dreams which wanted to believe they were coming true now, but her head knew that was not what was happening. Because she didn't see before her a man who wanted to get to know her again, who was looking at her with hope. She saw a man who was afraid that she was after his fortune, who was prepared to do anything to protect it.

She took a shaky step in the direction of the door. 'I shouldn't have come here. I'll instruct my solicitor to be in touch. Perhaps when *he* tells you that I want nothing from you, you'll believe it.'

He took a step towards her. 'You aren't curious to find out whether the sex between us is as good now as it was then?'

Libby's breath caught in her throat. She could smell the distinctive scent of him, which she'd always thought would sell by the ton if it could be bottled. But there was no way it could be, because it didn't contain any tangible ingredients. It was the smell of pure male heat, energy, virility, as potent as the first taste of mint on the tongue. It was overlaid with some expensive aftershave now, but she felt in danger of bursting into flames before she even got a whiff of that. And maybe she would have, if not for the cold douse of remembrance that she had never made him feel anything other than lukewarm in return.

'Come on, Rion, don't pretend I satisfied you in the bedroom any more than I satisfied you in any other area once we were married.'

He stared at her, almost unsure that he'd heard her correctly. Didn't she know that even now he was fighting to stop himself from lying her back against the desk and making her his in the most basic way there was? That, despite how far he'd come, she alone seemed to possess the unwelcome ability to remind him how unrefined he truly was?

'You think I'm *pretending*? Then stay. I can assure you I will take great pleasure in convincing you that I'm not.'

Libby shook her head. He was just trying to use her weakness for him against her. 'You can drop the act, Rion. I know you're only afraid that I'm after your money.'

'Oh, I am, am I?' He raised his eyebrows. 'Or do I just want to give our marriage a second chance?'

Libby swallowed hard, felt her heart begin to pound, felt it echo at her temples, 'No…I know you don't.'

'Well, if you're so sure then I guess this is it,' he said, his eyes never leaving hers as he swiftly slid the divorce papers back across the table towards her. 'But I don't doubt we'll be seeing plenty of each other in court. If you still intend to proceed, that is?'

'I—'

'You really ought to think very carefully about exactly what you want,' he cautioned, as he reached for a slip of paper from the inside drawer of his desk and scribbled down an address. 'I'm travelling to Metameikos on business tomorrow afternoon. Should you wish to join me, we leave from this airstrip at four.'

She did a double-take. 'Sorry?'

'I'm travelling to Metameikos tomorrow,' he repeated, handing her the slip of paper. 'Come with me and let me spend the next two weeks showing you why getting divorced isn't in the least bit logical. If I fail, then at the end I will sign.'

Libby's mouth dropped open in shock.

She'd been sure he'd only suggested trying again to protect his bank balance. But now…

'Even if… I can't—I'm supposed to be working out some potential new tours for next season before my first group arrives,' she stuttered.

Rion frowned. 'Tours?'

'It's my job,' she said, realising she'd never explained

what had brought her to Athens in the first place. 'I work for a company called Kate's Escapes.'

So she was working, he thought in surprise. In the tourist industry. That explained the tan, but not why. Surely Ashworth Motors *had* to have fallen on hard times. 'So come to Metameikos.' He shrugged. 'Work out a potential tour there. The scenery is the most beautiful in all of Greece.'

Libby's eyes widened even further.

'I…I—'

'Shouldn't make an impetuous decision, *gineka mou*,' he finished for her, striding forward and pinning back the door. 'Think about it. You have until tomorrow to decide.'

And with that he ushered her out of the door and closed it behind her.

Outside his office, Libby stood rooted to the spot, not sure she was capable of the neurological function required to make it down the stairs.

He'd said he wanted to see whether they could make their marriage work. Even more astounding than that, he'd asked her to go away with him, to work alongside him, in Metameikos.

They weren't the kind of statements that sounded particularly momentous. They didn't offer an answer to world peace or hint at a cure for some deadly disease. But to Libby they stopped her world on its axis and started it rotating in the opposite direction from the one in which it had been spinning for the last five years.

Because it showed her that he might be ready for

marriage now, in a way that neither of them had been before.

For never, in the three months they had spent together as husband and wife, had he seemed to want to spend time with her or share his work with her, and he'd only ever discouraged her from working. Nor had he ever really spoken of Metameikos, never mind suggested he had attachment enough to return to the place where he'd grown up.

Libby leaned back against the door, her memories surfacing like lava in a volcano disturbed.

No, from the day they'd arrived in Athens, his focus had always been on leaving the past behind him and making it on his own. And whilst she'd been delighted to escape her tyrannical father and leave her past behind too, she'd arrived with a head full of dreams. Dreams about living a life which didn't revolve around money and status, but love and freedom. But they'd barely finished saying their vows when he'd thrown himself into working eighteen-hour days. She'd virtually never seen him, and on the rare occasions when she had, all he'd done was talk about moving to a bigger apartment, putting money down on a house, finding an investor in his business idea.

At first Libby had admired his diligence. She knew very little about his childhood, but what she did know was that, unlike her, he'd grown up with nothing, on the poor side of Metameikos. It was understandable that getting another decent job was important to him—especially after the way her father had treated him—and she knew they couldn't survive on their wits alone.

But as he'd come home later and later every day, she'd found his obsession harder and harder and harder to cope with. Because she had known that simply working eight-hour days earned him enough to cover the rent and the bills, so why did he feel the need to work any more? If he loved her, wasn't spending his evenings and his weekends with her worth more than overtime pay?

It hadn't seemed to be. And as the weeks had passed she'd begun to wonder if he had ever really loved her at all. Because not only had it appeared to fail to cross his mind that a life spent isolated and alone, wondering if and when he was going to come home from work, was nothing like the life she'd imagined when she'd married him, but he hadn't even really talked to her about his job either—hadn't involved her in the very thing that had determined the course of her days. The same way it had been with her father and Ashworth Motors. Perhaps she could have dealt with that if they'd shared other things, but he'd never seemed to have time for anything else— save for lovemaking, late at night, when he came home. But he'd only ever seemed disappointed in that.

And eventually she'd had to admit to herself that she was disappointed with their marriage too. Yes, in marrying him she'd escaped the physical restrictions her father had placed on her, avoided marrying a suitor of his choosing, but being Mrs Delikaris hadn't really felt much different from being Miss Ashworth. She'd felt no more in control of her own life than she had before. What had happened to her chance to just be Libby?

It had disappeared, she had finally admitted to herself one day, three months after their wedding. And unless she did something about it, their marriage was going to destroy her.

He had been tying his tie in the bedroom the following morning, when she'd finally plucked up the courage. 'Rion, before you leave for work again there's something I want to talk to you about.'

'Oh?'

She took a deep breath. 'I've decided to apply for a job at the language school down the road.'

It wasn't going to solve all her problems, but it might be a start. She'd wanted to get a job ever since they'd arrived, for herself as well as to help out with paying the bills, but he'd told her it wasn't necessary. She realised now she should have fought harder.

'They're looking for native English-speakers to help with classes,' she continued, 'and I thought an extra bit of cash coming in might mean you needn't spend so much time working.'

He shook his head. 'I told you before, it's not necessary for you to get a job.'

She sucked in a frustrated breath. Couldn't he see that she *needed* a life of her own? 'But I want to. I'll be able to learn Greek whilst I'm there and—'

'I promised you a private tutor.' He looked pained. 'And you will have one—just as soon as I secure an investment.'

'But I don't want to wait that long. I can't even greet the neighbours!'

Rion's face contorted. 'I can assure you it won't be *that* long.'

She shook her head. 'Even so, it isn't just that. I want to go to a class, to meet other people.' Her shoulders dropped. 'When you're at work I just feel so…lonely.'

Rion blinked up at her. 'I am more than willing to have a child, if that is what you mean.'

Libby's eyes widened in disbelief. She'd always dreamed of having a family of her own one day, but not before she'd had the chance to really live herself, and certainly not now, when he was only suggesting having a baby as a solution to a problem.

A problem he didn't even understand. And was it really any wonder? No, she realised, feeling her heart rupture, he couldn't, because the truth was he didn't even know her. They'd married so hastily that she'd hadn't even had the time and space to get to know herself.

And in that instant Libby suddenly saw, as if a bolt of lightning had forked down from the sky and illuminated everything, that as long as she remained here she never would. That even if she stayed and fought and fought she would never really gain control of her own life. No, there was only one way to do that.

She shook her head. 'No, Rion, a child isn't what I want. I want—' She dropped her eyelids and took a deep breath. 'I don't know exactly what I want, but I know it isn't this. I…I don't want to stay here.'

And that was the moment she discovered for sure that she *was* just as big a disappointment to him as he had been to her.

Rion grimaced. 'Then go. I think we both know it's been on the cards from the start.'

Libby drew in a ragged breath, forcing her eyes open and blinking under the bright artificial lights of the corridor outside his office, remembering the twin feelings of both heartbreak and release as she'd walked away. She couldn't have gone on living that way. She had needed time to find herself, to take control of her life.

But now she had. And he was implying that he had too.

What was more, though it seemed so much *had* changed, her physical reaction to him most definitely hadn't. She breathed out deeply, listening to the sound of her heart, still racing. In a way that shocked her most of all, and to her shame it was undoubtedly the hardest thing to fight. Because she'd been convinced she'd never felt anything like it in the intervening years for the simple reason that she was no longer a young girl in the throes of her first love affair. The reality, it seemed, was that there was just no other man on earth who could make her whole body go into meltdown quite the same way that he did. Just by looking at her.

And, whilst she knew that instructing a solicitor to proceed with the divorce the hard way was the logical thing to do, she couldn't help it—her body longed for her to say yes. And so did her heart, because, no, they didn't know each other now, but what if they got to know one another and rediscovered what they'd once had before all that? Then divorcing him would be a huge mistake. So shouldn't she seize the chance to find out whether they could recapture it, even if the odds were minuscule and—?

Suddenly the ground gave way from under her, and she felt herself stumble backwards into hard, compacted muscle. As her mind played catch-up amongst the shock of lost footing and the treacherous thrill of arousal, she realised that to her enormous embarrassment Rion had just opened his office door. The one she'd been leaning against, with all of her weight. She leapt out of his arms, cheeks burning.

'I was just…' Libby exhaled, her mind completely blank. But then what excuse *was* there for being so utterly stupid as to remain leaning up against his door?

'Oh, no need to explain,' he said, his mouth quirking into a smile as he walked past her, his hands briefly brushing her sides as if to steady her. 'Happens all the time.'

He hit the button for the lift and the doors opened immediately. He gestured for her to join him, but she shook her head frantically.

'Until tomorrow, then,' he said with a grin.

And before Libby had time to protest that she still had twenty-four hours in which to decide, and that taking a breather before going downstairs didn't mean anything, the doors of the lift had already closed.

Which wouldn't have been half so frustrating if they hadn't both known he was right.

CHAPTER THREE

SHE'D had a whole sleepless night and the clarity of a morning in which to talk herself out if of it, but at three-thirty the following afternoon Libby found herself and her well-worn suitcase in a taxi on her way to the airstrip.

And she even seemed to be managing to sit still. For, although there was a part of her that *was* tempted to tell the driver to turn around and go as fast as he could in the opposite direction—the part which believed Rion had been far too cold in his office for this to end in anything other than heartache—over the course of the last twenty-four hours the rest of her had decided that going with Rion wasn't just following her heart and her hormones, it was logical.

Because unless she went with him she'd never fully be able to move on, and that had been half the point of her seeking to finalise their separation in the first place. The logic was the same as if she'd been handed a lottery ticket. She'd know the chances of it containing the winning numbers were tiny, but until she checked she'd never know, and every day she'd wake up with a voice whispering *what if?* in her ear.

Not that if they had an actual lottery ticket it would matter to Rion whether it bore the lucky numbers or not, Libby thought ruefully as they drove alongside a hangar and a sparkling white plane bearing the striking Delikaris Experiences logo taxied round in a semi-circle and stopped in front of them. Because she was fast coming to realise that in their years apart his obsession with personal success had taken on gargantuan proportions.

Which suggested that the more she got to know him, the more she'd discover that they were incompatible. It was obvious that he cared about nothing other than money if he had earned so much in five years, and, what was more, he'd clearly chosen to spend it on flashy possessions like his own private jet. If *she* had that volume of cash she'd head straight back out to Africa and do some good with it. She shook her head as she stepped out onto the tarmac. She'd once thought Rion was the antithesis of her father, but now she had to wonder if they'd been two sides of the same coin all along.

But it seemed owning a plane was not enough for Rion, Libby acknowledged ruefully as she looked up and saw that he was also piloting it. She watched with a dry mouth as he disappeared from the cockpit and re-appeared at the top of the steps, looking devastatingly sexy in a pair of dark aviator glasses and a casual white shirt with the cuffs rolled back, revealing his tanned forearms. Instinctively she reached up to undo the top button of her cotton blouse, feeling constricted.

'The thought of being back in my company making you hot under the collar already, *gineka mou*?' he asked dryly as he descended the steps to the satisfying sight of her waiting for him.

For a second inside his office—when she'd implied she had a titled lover waiting in the wings to marry her—there had been a small part of him which had wondered whether the combination of her desire for him, the promise of a private jet and the threat of lengthy court proceedings was enough to persuade her. But then he'd found her lingering outside, had felt her whole body ignite when she'd fallen against him, and he'd known for sure.

'I'm glad,' he added, 'but I'm afraid you will have to hold that thought. Although my autopilot mode is exceptionally sophisticated, I'm not sure it would be wise to join you in the cabin for the length of time I intend to spend making love to you.'

A shiver of pleasure rippled through her, but as soon as Libby clocked her automatic response she stopped it in its tracks, suddenly afraid. Daring to hope that he was serious about giving their marriage a second chance was one thing, but starting to believe he felt anything other than lukewarm in her presence was a different delusion altogether—a dangerous one. And suddenly she foresaw how easily he could trample all over her heart if she went into this with rose-tinted glasses on.

No, she was safest going into this from the standpoint that remaining married was irrational and that he was no more excited by her now than he had been during the months of their marriage. If he presented her with actual evidence to the contrary—well, that would be the time to re-evaluate her views.

'What's wrong with the cockpit?' she challenged audaciously.

Rion's eyes flared in shock. So, the innocent young girl he'd married was long gone, and in her place was an experienced adulteress, who only yesterday had been claiming she needed the divorce to move on with another man, and was now suggesting they make love at the earliest opportunity. To his infinite frustration his disgust was accompanied by the overwhelming urge to take her right here on the tarmac, and an erection so hard it was painful.

And it made him furious—because it seemed that no matter how *she* behaved, she still reminded him of *his* lack of refinement. She always had. He drew in a ragged breath. But at least he'd feel no shame taking her back to his house in Metameikos, no shame in flying her there on his plane. Unlike five years ago, after their pitiful wedding, when he'd been forced to take her on the bus back to that shabby rented apartment. He smarted in distaste. From the second he'd opened the front door of that place—the only one in Athens he'd been able to afford—all the self-belief that maybe he could be good enough for her had evaporated. He'd never felt more ashamed of who he was in his life.

And he knew she'd never felt more ashamed of him—she'd been so desperate to escape it, her lack of faith in him so unequivocal, that she'd even volunteered to work. But even though he'd done everything he could so that she didn't have to, even though he'd avoided involving her in the sordid details of his pathetic day job, worked every hour there was to try and save for their own place—a place she could be proud of—it had never been enough.

And it never will be, a voice inside him taunted, *even though you fought so hard for all this because you believed if you succeeded she'd come crawling back.*

No—that was a lie. That hadn't been the reason. His determination might have doubled the day she left, but he'd succeeded for himself, and for Jason, his brother.

He turned away from her, his voice terse. 'You will be travelling in the cabin.'

There wasn't any evidence to the contrary then, Libby acknowledged with ridiculous disappointment. She really didn't excite him. And the sooner he admitted it, the sooner she could silence the *what ifs*? She ducked down, pretending to look for another pair of legs on the opposite side of the plane. 'Because you have a co-pilot joining you up front?'

'No. I fly alone.'

She walked towards the steps defiantly. 'Then there is no reason why I shouldn't join you, is there?'

It was only when he'd followed her in and sat down beside her that she realised in fighting so hard to prove that he didn't really want her she'd just inadvertently guaranteed their close proximity for the duration of the flight.

'How long will it take us to get to Metameikos?' she asked hesitantly.

'Just under an hour.'

No time at all, she thought, trying to feel relieved as he hit the starter switch and took the controls. But they hadn't even taken off yet, and she was already transfixed by the sight of his long-fingered hands manoeuvring the complex equipment, unable to prevent herself remembering how they had once felt against her bare skin.

God, why did looking at him keep making her think about sex?

She moved awkwardly in her seat and tried to think of a logical answer. Maybe it was because he'd been the object of her first teenage crush, and somehow that made him the blueprint for the kind of man she found attractive. But, whilst his dark Mediterranean looks had been a novelty to her at fifteen, she'd met plenty of men since who fitted that description. The language teacher at the night classes she'd enrolled in as her first act of freedom once she'd arrived back in England; one or two of the other tour guides that Kate—whom she'd met at those language classes—had introduced her to when she'd expressed her enthusiasm for travel; the multitude of men she'd inevitably met the world over once she'd started filling in. But none of them had made her feel this irrepressible physical *hunger*.

Or maybe it was just that he was the only man she'd ever made love with, and like Pavlov's dogs, who had salivated when they heard bells ringing because they had come to associate that sound with food, her body had connected the sight of him and the smell of him with sex. Yes, that was probably it. She just needed to un-

condition her response, to associate him with something negative instead—the way he'd become so
obsessed with money, perhaps. She took a deep breath,
relieved to have alighted on a course of action that
would bring about an end to it.

'So, when did you learn to fly?' she asked, deciding
to lead the conversation down the 'needless luxury' route.

'Years ago, for research. Flying lessons were one of
the first gift experiences I decided to market, along with
luxury driving days,' he answered, handing her some
headphones as they approached the runway.

It was genius, Libby realised, for the first time contemplating *how* he'd made his money. He'd recognised
other people's dreams and found a way of offering them
neatly packaged in a box. But then that had always been
what he did best—it was what had once persuaded her
father to promote him from valet to salesman to showroom manager. He'd always known exactly which
element of an Ashworth motor to push, depending on
the customer and their body language. Speed and performance for men on the brink of a mid-life crisis; style
and sex-appeal for the computer geek who'd just earned
his first million; an investment opportunity for the
retired banker and safety features for his anxious wife.

But did his customers ever really get everything
they'd dreamed of? Or was the reality quite different?
Libby thought bleakly, unable to help making a com-
parison with their marriage as they took off.

Marrying Rion had been her dream from the very
first day she'd seen him—when she'd taken her father

some papers he'd forgotten and caught Rion looking up at her from the 1964 Ashworth Elite he'd been polishing with those devastating liquid brown eyes. She'd been so infatuated that it hadn't occurred to her that neither of them were ready for marriage, full-stop.

And it was no wonder she had felt that way really, she thought as they soared above Athens, the Parthenon shrinking to the size of a hotel on a Monopoly board below them. Because not only had he looked so different from the suitors her father had kept forcing her to meet, but when the furtive looks between them had eventually turned to snatched conversation on the days when her father was off-site, she'd discovered he *was* different. So unpretentious, and so exciting. He hadn't spent their conversations praising her father or calculating the acreage of the Ashworth estate; he'd talked to her about the travel books she liked to read, about the customs in Greece—which had seemed the most exotic place in the world to Libby, who'd never left Surrey, and whose long, monotonous days had been spent walled up inside Ashworth Manor and its grounds.

Libby felt a tightness around her wrists and her ankles at the memory of how her father had deemed even a walk to the village shops too much autonomy, even in her late teens. How her mother, plagued by the guilt her husband had made her feel for never producing a son, had enforced every rule he created.

And so her conversations with Rion had become a ritual, however infrequent, which she'd survived on for the duration of her teenage years. And though the details they'd actually shared with one another during those conversations had been sparse—he'd rarely spoken about his childhood, and never mentioned any family other than his mother, who'd brought him to England when he was in his early teens—at the time she'd only seen that lack of information as a positive. He'd obviously had no wish to discuss what must have been a difficult period in his life, and she had understood that, because she'd had no wish to talk about her childhood either.

The whole appeal of their conversations had been that they'd offered an escape from that—a freshly created world where nothing that had gone before mattered. And, although she'd never really been able to see a way in which marriage to him might be possible, nor imagine exactly how it might be if it was, she hadn't stopped dreaming about living in that world all the time.

Until one January day, not long after her nineteenth birthday, when she'd passed the showroom accidentally-on-purpose and found him actually waiting for her. He'd had a smile on his face so uncontainable that remembering it made her heart flip over even now.

'Rion, what is it?'

'Your father—he's promoted me. I'm going to be the showroom manager.'

'That's fantastic!' She beamed and threw her arms out, but just stopped short of embracing him, suddenly afraid that she might have imagined the significance of their conversations. Until he reached out and took her hands in his for the first time, and looked her straight in the eye.

'It means that I'm going to be on a really decent salary.'

She nodded enthusiastically, her hands shaking.

He took a deep breath. 'There's something I want to ask you. That I've wanted to ask you for a long time. Before I didn't think…but now…'

Libby's heart rose ten inches in her chest.

She heard his breath come thick and fast, his voice shaky. 'Would you consider marrying me, Liberty Ashworth?'

Her arms didn't hesitate this time. She threw them round him, and then he kissed her. The first and most magical kiss of her entire life.

'I know that technically I'm supposed to ask your father first, but—'

'No…this is perfect,' she breathed—because it was. The choice of who she married was hers, not anybody else's, and it meant the world to her that he understood that.

But her father didn't agree. When they went to ask for his blessing Thomas Ashworth fired Rion on the spot for his impudence.

'I have promoted you from valet to showroom manager in four short years and that is still not enough for you? How dare you consider yourself worthy enough to even *look* at my daughter? I try to nurture your talent for selling and this is how you repay me?' he spat. And then he made it clear to Libby that if she even tried to contact Orion again, he would banish her from the Ashworth family completely.

Her father had meant is as a threat, of course, but to Libby it had simply acted as an incentive. To swap her life of oppression for one of freedom. But it hadn't been until she and Rion had eloped to Athens that she'd realised she'd been utterly naïve to suppose they could go on living in that imaginary world, that marriage to anyone could have given her the autonomy she'd so desperately needed.

Libby drew in a ragged breath as the view from the aircraft window became more rural, and ran her hand through the short length of her hair, frustrated that she'd recalled the past in such damned fine detail again. But then she'd always had remarkable powers of recollection. It was a blessing in her job—that she remembered every travel guide she'd ever read was what had convinced Kate to take her on in the first place, when her practical experience had been non-existent—but it felt like a curse now.

'So, what business do you have in Metameikos?' she said loudly above the noise of the plane, determined to distract herself from remembering any more.

She saw the edge of his lip curl in amusement. 'For a minute there I thought the cat had got your tongue.' He paused over the English phrase, as if it amused him to remember one so fitting. 'What were you thinking about?'

'Nothing in particular.'

'No? I could have sworn you were looking at my hands, remembering how it felt to have them touch you.'

Colour flooded her cheeks. 'So you're a mind-reader *and* a pilot? Is there no end to the talents you've acquired in the last five years?'

'I wasn't reading your mind, *gineka mou*, I was reading your body.'

All too aware that he was an expert at that, Libby reverted to her original choice of subject. 'So, what business *do* you have in Metameikos?'

'I have some meetings to attend, some functions at which I need to make an appearance. Plus there are some things I need to sort out at my property before I settle there permanently.'

Libby was so surprised by this information that she let the frankly detailless description of his business go unchallenged. He'd barely mentioned Metameikos in the past, let alone expressed any desire to return there permanently.

'You are making Metameikos your home? I always presumed it didn't mean that much to you.'

Rion's lips barely moved. 'It's a business decision.'

'But your main offices are in Athens, aren't they?'

'Indeed.'

Libby frowned. That he'd as good as stated he had no emotional attachment to the place came as no surprise to her—especially now that it appeared he had no emotional attachment to anything other than money—but then why move there? She didn't know a great deal about Metameikos, compared with her detailed knowledge of many other parts of the world, but she did know that it was no Athens when it came to its business credentials. What she *could* recall was that it was Greece's only independent province and that it was pretty much divided in two—one half being one of the poorest areas of the whole country, where she knew Rion had grown up, whilst the other was full of luxury holiday homes belonging to the very wealthy. If she remembered correctly, it was best known for a well-preserved ancient amphitheatre somewhere in the middle. There were no prizes for guessing which side they were heading to now, but why he planned on staying there permanently was a mystery.

'I hope to have an office in Metameikos too, soon.'

Libby nodded, but remained unconvinced. She supposed if he was branching out into all aspects of the leisure industry then the location was a desirable one for watersports and the like, but it still puzzled her. Maybe it was some kind of tax haven. 'Your meetings these next couple of weeks are related to that, then?'

'Indirectly,' he replied vaguely. 'This evening we will attend a play at the amphitheatre there.'

'A play?' she repeated back at him in astonishment, surprised not only that his time would be spent on something other than crunching numbers, but also that he wanted her to join him.

Rion gritted his teeth. So, she thought a man like him wasn't capable of enjoying a little culture. 'How is it that you are so adamant we lay the past to rest, when it is perfectly obvious you will never forget mine?'

She frowned. 'What do you mean by that?'

'I mean that much has changed.'

'Has it?' she asked, a flicker of hope igniting in her heart as the plane touched down, his landing utterly flawless.

'Why don't you see for yourself?' he asked, inclining his head towards the extensive property spanning the horizon. 'We're here.'

CHAPTER FOUR

OF COURSE, he only meant much had changed in terms of the kind of house he now owned and the kind of car he now drove, Libby thought dejectedly as they headed away from the airstrip towards the property in the distance, in his top-of-the-range Bugatti—the only car on the planet, if her memory served her correctly, that was worth more than the 1958 Ashworth Liberty. The car her father had named her after in the single greatest irony of her life.

But, although all signs pointed towards Rion's home being some equally extravagant and overstated villa on the more affluent side of Metameikos, when he rolled the car to a halt outside, she discovered to her surprise that it was not.

It was a period house built of stone, and had two different levels with steps running between them that were covered in terracotta pots overflowing with flowers. There were charming wooden shutters at the windows, and although the grounds were extensive, the house itself wasn't oppressively huge or ostentatious in any way. It looked like the perfect family home. What was more, if she'd ascertained things correctly during the drive here, it was situated pretty much *in between* the affluent side and the less privileged side of the province, just in front of the impressively preserved amphitheatre—which must have been the structure she had seen from the runway.

'What made you choose here?' she breathed, running her hand over the stonework, convinced he'd say he hadn't picked it out himself at all, but that when the need to relocate had arisen he'd left the selection of his accommodation up to an employee.

Rion paused for a moment, remembering how he and Jason had sat at the top of the amphitheatre, looking down at the house and the well-off family who had called it home. Owning it one day had been his only life goal then. Until Jason's death. Until she'd left him. He answered gruffly, 'As a kid, it was the house I always swore I'd own one day.'

He indicated for her to follow him in but Libby stalled on the threshold, astonished not only to discover that he *did* seem to have some attachment to Metameikos, but that for one of the first times ever he'd just given her a glimpse into his childhood.

Rion looked back over his shoulder to find her hovering on the doorstep. 'It's a little late to be having second thoughts about our arrangement now, *gineka mou.*'

'I'm not,' she said quickly, and then wished she hadn't sounded so sure about it. 'I was just admiring the house.'

And having second thoughts of a different nature, no

doubt, Rion thought cynically as she admired the décor of the hall. Like why she hadn't demanded half of everything he owned in her precious petition for divorce.

'I never expected it to be so…I don't know…'

But before she could find the right word to complete her sentence they both heard footsteps.

Rion turned and walked to the bottom of the staircase. 'Eurycleia.' He smiled warmly.

Libby looked up to see a woman who must have been in her mid-sixties descending the stairs, duster in hand.

Rion tilted his head upwards and switched into Greek. 'The house looks fantastic.' He shook his head ruefully. 'I hope you have not been working here all day.'

The old woman's eyes twinkled as she reached the second to last step, which put her on a level height with Rion. She placed her hands on the sides of his head in a motherly gesture and kissed him on the forehead. 'You know it's my pleasure. Welcome back.'

She raised her eyes then, and caught sight of Libby for the first time. 'Orion Delikaris,' she said, swiping him with the duster. 'Are you so rude that you are going to leave your guest just standing there, without even introducing us?'

Rion sighed and shook his head in an affectionate gesture which said *Well, I would have if you'd given me the chance.* 'Libby,' he said, beckoning her over, 'this is Eurycleia, my housekeeper and a dear old friend. Eurycleia, I'd like you to meet Libby…' He paused. 'My wife.'

Eurycleia's eyes widened, and then she gasped in

delight, clapped her hands together and rushed over to greet Libby with a kiss on both cheeks.

It took Libby completely by surprise. Not Eurycleia's benevolent welcome, but the way Rion had introduced her. It had been perfectly obvious in Athens that he'd never mentioned he had a wife, and she hadn't supposed he'd planned on changing that now. Because surely if word got out that he was married it would be unpleasantly public for him if it didn't work out? Unless… unless he was really that certain that it would?

Libby ignored the blood pounding in her ears at the thought. If Eurycleia was an old friend whose confidence could be trusted, it didn't count. She switched into Greek herself. 'It's a pleasure to meet you, Eurycleia.'

Rion's head shot up in surprise, but he didn't say a word.

'Beautiful *and* clever.' Eurycleia gave another delighted gasp, but before Libby could deny any such thing, Rion interrupted.

'Thank you, Eurycleia, for all you hard work. But I'm afraid Libby and I do not have long to refresh ourselves before we must attend the play this evening. Will you leave us now?'

Eurycleia looked inexplicably serious, as if he'd just announced he had to prepare to go to war. 'Of course you must. I will just collect my things and then I'll be gone.' She touched Rion's arm on her way past. 'There are some fresh honey and walnut biscuits in the kitchen, if either of you are peckish.'

'Thank you,' Rion said gratefully. 'And perhaps if

you wouldn't mind taking the next couple of weeks off—paid, of course. You'll understand, I'm sure, that Libby and I would like some time alone.'

Eurycleia looked momentarily hurt, but then nodded respectfully and began to scuttle back upstairs.

'Spend some extra time with that toy-boy of yours,' Rion chuckled after her, lightening the mood.

Eurycleia threw her hands exasperatedly in the air and turned back to Libby. 'He is three years younger than me—sixty-two!' She clicked her tongue at Rion. 'You make it sound as if he is twenty!'

Libby smiled after her, but the second Eurycleia had turned the corner at the top of the stairs she followed Rion into the open plan kitchen/living room and her face became solemn. 'I hardly think dismissing her altogether was necessary.'

Rion scowled, completely misinterpreting her meaning. 'No? You mean so long as you have someone to wait on you hand and foot you don't care whose sensibilities you might offend?'

She blinked, baffled. 'You mean if Eurycleia realises our marriage isn't what it seems?'

'No, Libby. I mean if Eurycleia walks in and finds us making love in the shower, or on the kitchen table, or sprawled out on the rug—'

Libby's heart-rate rocketed, and she fought to stop her mind from filling with all the erotic images he'd just conjured. 'Just because you are technically my husband it doesn't mean you *have* to make love to me, Rion.'

Rion searched her eyes for proof that she was just

feigning naïveté again. But he couldn't see it. He stood back and regarded her thoughtfully. Was it possible that she *really* believed he didn't want her? Yes, he realised suddenly, maybe it was. Because a man who possessed any integrity *wouldn't* want a wife who didn't think him good enough, who'd run away, who was guilty of infidelity. He gave a bitter snort of laughter. It had to be the only time she'd ever over-estimated him.

'No,' he growled, 'I *shouldn't* want you. But my body doesn't give a damn about that.'

Libby eyed him doubtfully, but before she had time to wonder if there was a strand of truth in his words he showed her, placing his hands around the small of her waist and drawing her so close to his body that she could feel the hard shaft of his erection against her belly.

'Now are you convinced?' he murmured.

Liquid heat began to pump through her veins. She forced herself to step backwards, but he hauled her against his body again, placed one long finger under her chin and tilted it upwards, forcing her to look into his eyes.

'I want you.'

No, it wasn't possible. She knew it wasn't because— Libby searched his face for the look of indifference she'd read on his face every day of their marriage, every time they'd made love.

But she couldn't see it now.

She blinked hard and searched again.

She still couldn't see it, because unless she was mistaken it wasn't there. All she could see was what looked like red-hot need.

'And I know you don't want to, but you do still want me, don't you, Libby?' he whispered raggedly, lowering his head so that his mouth was so agonisingly close she could feel the heat of his breath against her lips.

'I…' Her breath caught in her throat as he stroked the finger he had been resting beneath her chin across her shoulderblade and down the side of her body, so that the backs of his knuckles grazed the side of her breast. Her nipples tightened to unbearable peaks. 'I—'

'I'll be off, then—oh, I'm sorry.'

Libby and Rion sprung apart as Eurycleia stuck her head around the door of the living room and then beat a hasty retreat.

Rion left Libby reeling in the middle of the room and strode towards the door, utterly shameless. 'Thank you, Eurycleia. Enjoy your time off.'

'I'm sure I will.' She nodded, hurrying towards the front door with an embarrassed wave goodbye.

Rion closed the door behind her and turned back to Libby. 'Now do you see why dismissing Eurycleia is a good idea, *gineka mou?*'

Libby could feel her chest rising and falling, but her mind was too hazy with desire and disbelief to speak. Was it possible that he did really want her? She had sworn she wouldn't let herself even imagine it until she had evidence, but what had that been, if not solid proof?

Rion flicked a look down at his watch. 'Much as I would gladly finish *proving* why, I'm afraid it will have to keep another few hours,' he drawled. 'The play starts in forty-five minutes. I presume you wish to change?'

Libby looked down at her crumpled blouse, her mind racing. The play. His desire. How many other things had changed too? She nodded.

'The bathroom is the second door on the right at the top of the stairs. Be ready to leave in twenty-five minutes.'

She'd showered, changed into a gypsy-style dress, and been ready to go in even less time that that, but three-quarters of an hour later, as they settled down on the cushions and blankets which had been laid out to make the stone seats of the *theatron* more comfortable, she only wished her mind was as settled. Because now Eurycleia wasn't the only one he'd told about her. He'd just introduced her as his wife to the man who'd shown them to their seats, and to the elderly couple next to them too.

Once the play had started—an adaptation of Homer's *Odyssey* by the local drama group—and the hubbub of the audience had been replaced with tranquillity, she couldn't go on denying what that meant. She'd wanted evidence that he was for real, that he *did* want to give their marriage another shot, that recapturing what they'd once had before everything had changed might be possible. And, even though she'd thought the chances of that were minuscule, he'd given it to her. He'd given her hope.

And it was both exhilarating and terrifying. Because she wanted to open her heart to it, to revel in it, but there was still so much they didn't know about each other, so many ways they might not be compatible, and deep down she knew it was too soon, too dangerous, too easy to be seduced by the romance of it all. The sky growing dark, the stars beginning to twinkle above them. The stars of Orion's belt, which always reminded her of him no matter where in the world she was, even though until yesterday she'd been convinced that looking up at the constellation which bore his name was the closest she'd ever get to him again.

Just as it was too easy to be seduced by the way he'd placed a blanket around her shoulders and left his hand lingering there as the players re-enacted the moment at the end of Odysseus's adventures when he and his wife Penelope were reunited after many years apart.

But not until they had each tested one another and banished their doubts, Libby thought, the play's pertinence far from lost on her. If she hadn't known better, she would have sworn that it was no accident. But hadn't he been planning on coming here alone before she'd even arrived in his office yesterday? Yes, Eurycleia's reaction when he'd mentioned the play tonight had proved that he had.

It had to be a coincidence, then, or simply that the ancient epic was full of such universal truths that it resonated in one way or another with everyone, as stories that stood the test of time always did. Yes, Rion was probably sitting beside her identifying with a totally different part. Like Odysseus's need to make his journey alone, or something.

Like Odysseus's need to make his journey alone? she repeated in her mind. *Before being reunited with his wife?*

Libby stole a sideways glance at his profile. Could it be possible that *was* what he was thinking? That when they'd married he'd been too young, that what he'd needed then was the space to make his own way in the world first, just as she had? And could he be thinking that he was ready for marriage now, and that the feelings which had drawn them together in the first place had never really gone away?

Suddenly the audience broke into rapturous applause. Libby's mind had been so far away that the sound made her jump, but she quickly recomposed herself and joined in enthusiastically, afraid that if he noticed her distractedness he might start asking questions she wasn't ready to answer. Not yet.

As the actors took their bows and filed off the stage, Rion stood and led the way down the stone steps. The street outside, which had contained just a few people carrying tables when they'd arrived, was now full of stalls, selling every kind of food and drink imaginable.

'The performance is just the first part of the local *panigiria*,' he explained. 'The rest of the celebrations will go on into the early hours of the morning.' He walked up to one of the stalls, exchanged pleasantries with the old man serving, and then ordered them two small glasses of golden liquid. 'This is the local liquor, sweetened with honey. Try it.'

'Thank you.' Libby accepted the glass and took a sip. Trying local food and drink had always been one of her favourite parts of travelling. Guidebooks filled with photos had given her an idea about the way different places looked ever since she'd begun devouring them in her childhood, but discovering how a place tasted was something you could never know until you'd been.

'It's delicious.'

He nodded. 'Come, I'd very much like to introduce you to someone.'

Would he? Her heart blossomed ridiculously in her chest.

'His name is Georgios,' he said, surveying the crowd. 'He's the Mayor.'

For a moment Libby felt staggered that he should know someone so prominent—until it occurred to her that he was now probably the most famous resident of Metameikos himself. But just as Rion appeared to spot Georgios in the crowd, and moved his hand to her elbow to guide her forward, a loud voice thundered behind them.

'Ah, Delikaris. I might have known you wouldn't pass up *this* opportunity.'

Libby turned round to see that the voice belonged to a large man with a balding head and an incongruously thick moustache.

'Spyros.' Rion inclined his head civilly, but Libby could hear the hostility in his voice. If Spyros heard it too, he didn't take the hint.

'I'm glad to see you're making use of the stalls *I* granted permission for this evening.' He dropped his eyes to their glasses.

'You mean the stalls belonging to men who have traded here every year for decades, but who now have to line *your* pockets for the privilege?' Rion ground out bitterly.

Spyros gave an unpleasant laugh. 'For the good of the

community at large. I only grant permission to those whose produce meets health and safety standards.'

'Which all of them did before, because they don't sell anything they wouldn't feed to their own families.'

'Well, we'd all like that to be the case, but you can never be too careful these days. It's important to know exactly who you're dealing with. Talking of which…' Spyros ran his eyes lecherously over Libby. 'I don't believe we've been introduced.'

The tops of Libby's arms broke out into goose pimples and she stroked her hands over them, wishing she hadn't had to leave the blanket that Rion had placed around her shoulders in the amphitheatre.

'This is Libby,' Rion said reluctantly.

'Libby,' Spyros repeated, so lewdly that for the first time in her life she hated the shortened form of her name even more than the extended version.

He turned back to Rion. 'Decided on a change of tack, eh? Why keep your lovers behind closed doors when everyone knows you have a different one for every day of the week? Your honesty is gutsy, I'll give you that. Or is it just a sign that you've already accepted defeat?'

Libby frowned, wondering what the hell he was talking about, but her mind was too full of the nauseating image of seven scantily clad women labelled Monday through to Sunday to even hazard a guess.

'I'm afraid not—for your sake,' Rion said between gritted teeth. 'As it happens, Libby is my wife.'

To Libby's surprise, Spyros looked from her to Rion and then let out a guffaw of laughter. 'It's imaginative,

I'll give you that. But surely you don't think even this lot will fall for it?' He signalled to the crowds of people enjoying the festivities and then turned to Libby. 'So, tell me, how much does it pay, playing the part of his wife? Handsomely, I hope. Sex and politics *are* the two oldest professions in the world, after all.'

The cords in Rion's neck went taut, and he raised himself to his full height, but before he could take another step forward Libby cut in front of him. She didn't know what the hell was going on, but Spyros's condescension and disrespect was such an unpleasantly vivid reminder of her father that she couldn't remain silent.

'I'm not sure what business it is of yours, but I can assure you that we *are* married.'

Rion looked at her, and she saw something flare in his eyes. She wasn't sure whether it was pride or horror.

'Don't tell me he actually convinced you to go through with it? Do you *really* think people are stupid enough to believe that he's capable of some whirlwind romance, that overnight he's become a family man? All it screams is rashness and irresponsibility.'

'You think so?' Rion said, pretending to ponder the concept. 'Lucky, then, that Libby and I married five years ago.'

He paused to watch Spyros's face drop before continuing, 'We have been apart for a period of time, yes, but what marriage doesn't go through bad patches?' He looked critically at him. 'I'd say those that seem *not* to are the ones which invite suspicion.'

Spyros's conceited expression turned to one of pure

malevolence. 'You will not win this, Delikaris—' he twisted his head and glowered at the crowd '— You're no better than they are.'

'No, I don't believe I am,' Rion replied. 'And that's the difference between us.'

Rion fought the urge to show Spyros that wasn't the only difference between them, that if he ever insulted his wife again he would pay, but he knew that would only be living up to the creep's preconceptions. Instead he placed his hand on Libby's arm, momentarily wished he could repress his rudimentary urges with such ease when it came to her, then encouraged her forward and smiled with intentionally nauseating civility. 'Now, if you'll excuse us, we were just off to see Georgios.'

Libby watched as Spyros angrily pushed his way back through the crowd to a small, grubby-looking man and a large woman in a gaudy peacock-print dress whom she presumed must be his wife. Her nose was turned up at two young boys acting out the fight between Odysseus and the Cyclops, one with one eye tightly shut, the other brandishing a rolled-up theatre programme, creating clouds of dust.

Libby would have cheered them on if she hadn't felt as if she'd just been engulfed by a dust cloud herself. A dust cloud which, once settled, she had a horrible feeling might reveal a truth she didn't want to see. She turned her head back to face Rion, who had the audacity to be scanning the crowd for the Mayor again.

'Would you care to tell me what just happened?'

'Sorry?'

'That man—Spyros, or whatever his name is—who is he?' *And who are you?*

'He's the current leader of Metameikos,' Rion replied through gritted teeth.

As he spoke she pieced together the bits of information she'd gleaned from their conversation. 'And what? You're standing against him in some sort of election?'

As she said the words aloud, she knew she'd hit the nail on the head before he even had the chance to nod. *That* was why Eurycleia had been so reverential when he'd mentioned coming here tonight—*that* was why he wanted her to meet the Mayor—that was why—

Libby felt as if the fragile threads keeping her heart suspended in her chest had just been cut.

That was the real reason why he'd refused to sign the divorce petition and invited her here. Not because he wanted to give their marriage another shot. But because he thought that playing the family man in the local community for a couple of weeks might win him a few extra votes.

'And you just didn't think you'd bother mentioning it?' Libby exploded, almost as angry at herself for thinking he might have changed as at the concrete proof that he didn't give a damn about anyone but himself.

'Do you mind if we don't do this in front of the whole of Metameikos?' he said under his breath, steering her away from the throng of people who had started to turn around.

Libby shook him off angrily. 'Oh, no, it wouldn't do for your wife to make a scene, would it?'

'Not over nothing, no,' he said matter-of-factly, as if *she* was the one who was being unreasonable. 'This isn't a secret, it's a public election, *gineka mou*. I'm sorry if you didn't realise I was running but, given that you've been gone for five years, unfortunately there will be some things we don't know about each other.'

She raised her head to look at him, standing so righteously with the amphitheatre behind him. He looked like Alexander the Great, and in that instant she hated him. 'I don't care if there are a million things I don't know about you, Rion. I care about being lied to, about being used as an accomplice to deceive others without even knowing about it.'

He gave a sceptical laugh. 'Are you protesting for the innocent people of Metameikos, or for yourself?'

'Both.'

'Spyros is corruption personified, as his father was before him. He runs this province on lies. I hardly think I'm doing the people of Metameikos a disservice by turning up to a play with my wife.'

'You still deceived *me*. You told me you didn't want to sign the divorce papers because you wanted to see whether now there could be a second chance for us.'

He shook his head. 'Indeed—and I do. That this fortnight happens to coincide with the election is irrelevant.'

Fury almost choked her. 'Then it won't affect your plans if I leave, will it?'

'Affect my plans? Not in the least.' He smiled disparagingly. 'But I'm afraid it may affect yours, since I won't be signing the divorce papers unless you stay.'

CHAPTER FIVE

'You blackmailing bastard,' she breathed, flinging out her arms in disgust and walking back along the dusty road which led to the house.

Much as she would have liked to lead him back to the growing frivolity of the *panigiria*, so that the whole of Metameikos could hear how emotionally backward he was, she needed the open space.

'There's no need to be upset, *gineka mou*,' he said, catching up with her in two easy strides. 'The agreement was that we would spend two weeks finding out whether our marriage could work, and I still have every intention of proving to you that it can.'

Good God, the lies tripped off his tongue so easily. 'So you're just going to go on pretending that you want me because keeping me here is beneficial to your campaign?'

'Don't lecture *me* about pretending,' he growled, catching her wrist in his hand and spinning her round to face him. 'You can tell yourself whatever you want— that I don't want you, that you don't want me, that you're being faithful to this lover you've got waiting in

the wings—but we both know what's happening between us…that if we hadn't been interrupted it would
have happened already.'

He gave her no time to assemble her defences. The
instant she realised what was happening his lips were
already on hers, hungry, demanding, urgent. And, before
she could even think about whether it was wise or not,
her body had already kicked into its natural response:
to kiss him with the same intensity right back.

It *wasn't* the least bit wise, of course, but by the time
she'd reached that conclusion the voice of reason in her
mind was inaudible, obscured by the heady release of
five years of deeply buried need. Desire exploded in her
belly as he crushed her to him, as he tangled his hand
in her hair and angled her face upwards so that he could
explore her mouth even more thoroughly. And she let
it, because just for one moment she wanted to believe
that at least something about the last twenty-four hours
had been real.

For a nanosecond, as she compared the force of his
passion now with that of her memories, she actually
gave headroom to the possibility that it could be—that,
yes, he did want to rule half the world as well as owning
it, but maybe he wanted *her* too.

Yet just as that thought echoed through her mind, so
too did his words: *you can tell yourself whatever you
want…that you're being faithful to this lover you've got
waiting in the wings…* And immediately the bubble burst.

Oh, Rion wanted her, all right, but not because he'd
suddenly realised she was what he wanted. He'd carried

on believing she wanted this divorce in order to marry another man, and the thought of someone else having her was like a red rag to a bull. Not out of genuine jealousy, but because the chance to prove he could turn her on more than any other man turned *him* on. It was a challenge, another contest to be won.

Libby wrenched herself out of his embrace, the realisation like being doused with cold water.

'I have no lover,' she shot out suddenly.

She knew it was bound to invite a thousand questions, but it was the only way to eradicate this danger.

Rion eyed her skeptically, and looked down at the space she'd created between them. 'Do you think that if you start pretending he doesn't exist now, you can avoid the possibility of him finding out about this?'

Libby shook her head in vain. 'Do *you* think that if I did have a lover I'd betray him by coming here in the first place?'

Rion didn't know what the hell to think, but he did know her use of the word *betray* was the admission he had been waiting for. 'So you're confessing that your thoughts about me *have* been lustful ever since you walked into my office, *gineka mou*?'

'The only thing I'm confessing is that I would never have allowed myself to be seen in public as your wife if doing so humiliated anyone other than me.'

Rage flared in his eyes. 'Oh, yes, if only you'd married someone less *humiliating*, someone as refined and morally seamless as you are—oh, no, wait a minute. Haven't you, who has just spent the last ten minutes accusing me of omitting the truth, been lying about this other man all along?'

Libby's cheeks started to burn. 'You assumed—'

'In the same way that you *assumed* my business here had to do with Delikaris Experiences. Only you went one step further by perpetuating your lie.' His eyes narrowed. 'Why?'

She dropped her head. 'I thought it would make you see the logic in signing the divorce papers. You seemed sure that all I wanted was money, and I needed you to see that it wasn't.'

'Even though all the time it *was*?' he bellowed.

'No, I told you—'

'Oh, yes, you told me—getting a divorce now is *logical*. But you've already lived with the *humiliation* of being my wife for five years, so why did remaining married suddenly become *illogical*? Has Ashworth Motors folded? Is that it?' he went on. 'Are you here because you hope a hefty divorce pay-out will restore your family's fortunes, prevent you from having to work a day more?'

Libby drew in a ragged breath and began walking back in the direction of the house. How had she spent even a minute believing he was capable of understanding a single thing about her? He wasn't the Rion she'd once known. He'd grown so cynical. She glanced at him as he came alongside her. Why was that, when in the years since she'd been gone it appeared that so much had gone his way?

'I love my work,' she said tonelessly. 'And I've

already told you I don't want your money. After all this time I just thought it was the right thing to do. As for Ashworth Motors, I honestly have no idea. The last time I saw my parents was the day we left for Athens together, so your guess is as good as mine.'

'Your father refused to have you back?' He looked appalled.

'I didn't *go* back.' Didn't Rion realise she'd had nothing to go back to?

'So where did you go?'

'The first flight back to the UK from Athens landed in Manchester.' She shrugged. 'It seemed as good a place as any.'

It had been two hundred miles away from her parents for a start. Not that that had stopped her father getting hold of her phone number three years later, when he'd read about Rion's success in the paper and thought it was in his interest to call her and repent.

'So living alone in a strange city was preferable to being married to me?'

Libby's expression grew taut. 'It was what I needed to do, Rion. In the same way that I knew you were happier working, making it on your own.'

Rion turned sharply to look at her as they reached the front door. 'Happier? The only reason I was always working was to earn enough to get us out of that hovel we were living in!'

Libby felt as if someone had just removed the ground from beneath her feet. Working so hard had been his dream, hadn't it? After the excitement of getting married had gone, when she'd realised that she wanted to take control of her life, *he'd* discovered that what he really wanted was to make a success of himself alone. Hadn't he?

'It made you happier than I could, Rion. Our marriage wasn't what either of us was expecting. You said yourself the day I left it had been on the cards from the start.'

'Only because you never believed in me.'

Libby clung on to the front wall of the house for support, guilt washing over her in a wave. Was that true? *Had* she been the only one who'd been disappointed in their marriage? Her mind traced back over those three short months. No, whatever he said, she knew he had been too. But the reality was she was the one who'd given up on it altogether, who'd left her proud Greek husband. And suddenly she saw with hideous clarity the answer to her question. *Why* had he become the dark, jaded man stood before her now when so much had gone his way in the intervening years? Because she'd walked away from him.

Hot tears pricked behind Libby's eyes. 'I always believed in you, Rion, that's why I married you.'

Rion gritted his teeth. Yes, when she'd accepted his proposal she'd *believed* in him, believed her father would give them his blessing. And maybe she'd desired him so much that even after her father had given them the opposite she'd allowed herself to believe he was still *someone* back in Greece. She'd gone through with the wedding, after all. But once he'd taken her back to that god-awful apartment he'd known she must realise that he was really no one at all.

And, though he'd tried to convince himself that she didn't think like that, deep down he'd been half expecting her to bolt from the minute he'd carried her over the threshold.

He grimaced. God knew why he'd persisted in hoping she was immune to the same prejudices as her father even at that point. Or why, before that, he'd believed Thomas Ashworth was any different from Spyros and his father. He supposed he'd been blinded by gratitude because he'd given him his first proper job, because he'd been on the first step of the ladder to becoming the kind of man he'd sworn he'd become: a man whose life *was* worth something. A man whose family—mother, wife, child one day—would never have to suffer what Jason had.

But even so he shouldn't have been blind, should have recognised that the only reason her father had promoted him was because he made him more money than all his other Ashworth Motors employees put together. Should have realised it wasn't the mark of respect he'd taken it to be, that there was no way on earth Thomas Ashworth would even consider accepting someone like him as his son-in-law and successor to his company.

Not that Rion had ever wanted the latter. He'd always planned to build his own company the second he'd earned enough to go solo. But Libby—from the first time she'd looked at him with those wide blue eyes which hadn't seemed to see any difference between them at all, he'd never been able to help wanting her. Even though they'd really known so little about one another, even though he'd always felt like a boy from the slums compared to her elegance and beauty, even though he should have known she was out of his league. He'd wanted her regardless—more than he'd ever wanted anything else in his life.

His eyes roamed over her. He hated the feeling of weakness. Wished that now he knew the look in her eyes was a lie, that she *was* just the same as her father, the wanting would disappear. It never had. Maybe it would when he took her again, one final time, with the full force of his need. Maybe it never would. But at least he was not in any danger of ever being so gullible again, of falling for her lies—so carefully engineered to absolve herself of blame.

'Well, if you've always believed in me so unfalteringly, and now you've had the time to *find yourself,* what could be better than two weeks discovering whether our marriage can work, just as we agreed?'

Libby shook her head desolately. 'Because you only want me for the good of your campaign!'

'I've already told you. The fact that your return happens to coincide with this election is just a fortunate coincidence. Allow me to spend two weeks convincing you this marriage can work, just as we agreed. If I fail, then I will sign the divorce papers.'

Her voice choked. 'I already know this marriage can't work. You've changed too much.'

She missed his wince. 'But we agreed that I had two weeks.' He looked at his watch patronisingly, knowing she was only so outraged at the prospect of staying now that she knew about the election because it meant there'd be no chance of her keeping their marriage—so shameful in her eyes—a secret.

'I'm afraid it's only been a matter of hours.'

Libby pressed the heels of her hands into the sockets of her eyes. She wanted to run away as far as possible, so she didn't have to face being blackmailed by the only man she'd ever loved, so she could forget this whole sorry episode had ever happened. She wanted to shake him until the old Rion rose to the surface, understood her, saw what he was doing was wrong, told her she wasn't the one who had done this to him. But she knew that was like wishing for sunshine at midnight. That even if she ran she'd never forget. He'd never let her, because he'd drag her through the courts indefinitely.

Which left only one option. She dropped her hands and raised defiant eyes to meet his.

'Then it seems you leave me with little choice. But I can assure you you'll live to regret not agreeing to this divorce while you had the chance.'

She turned quickly, to deny him the satisfaction of looking her in the eye and giving some gloating response. But as she picked up her small suitcase, which she'd dumped in the hallway earlier, and began walking up the stairs, she felt his gaze rake over her rear view and decided a snide comment would have been preferable. Because she knew it wasn't real, and that hurt most of all.

Rion sensed her telling hesitation and smiled, enjoying the sight of her bottom and her shapely legs. 'I doubt that either of us is going to regret being back in one another's company for two weeks, Liberty. The master bedroom is the third on the right, if you'd rather just cut to the chase and admit it.'

Libby swung round at the top of the stairs, her eyes blazing furiously. 'Libby,' she ground out. 'And the divorce petition is right here,' she replied, whipping it out of the front pocket of her suitcase and tossing it down the stairs, 'if *you'd* rather just rediscover your conscience.' And with that she stormed into the first room at the top of the stairs and slammed the door behind her.

Rion gathered up the papers and smirked to himself. She'd just shut herself in his storage room, and something told him that bedding down for the night amongst a heap of clutter he hadn't got round to sorting yet wasn't exactly the alternative to the master bedroom she'd had in mind.

Not that he had any idea what was really going on in her mind, he thought, turning at the foot of the stairs and trying to get his head around her revelation that she had no duke or earl waiting in the wings to marry her after all.

He walked into his study, tossed the papers into the bottom drawer of his desk, slammed it shut, and poured himself a generous measure of Scotch. It made little difference, of course; he was under no illusion about that. She'd still no doubt had other lovers, still found the idea of being married to *him* abhorrent, no matter how hard she tried to absolve herself of guilt by arguing that she'd simply needed time to 'find herself'.

He swilled the amber liquid around his glass. But what it did mean was that if she'd been pursued by men she deemed suitable husband material—and he had no doubt that she had been—in one way at least they hadn't matched up to him.

Was that why she'd never gone back to her parents?

Discovering that she hadn't had shocked the hell out of him at first, but then maybe she'd known that her father would require appeasement in the form of a second, more appropriate match. And maybe she hadn't been able to bear that thought, because she understood that, ironically, the kind of man she wanted fathering her children was not the kind of man who turned her on.

Rion lifted the glass to his lips and knocked back the measure in one go. It appalled him that his wife had been out there alone, that her father was such an unforgiving man that she'd felt unable to go back home. He'd gathered that Thomas Ashworth was a strict father even before they'd naïvely gone to seek his blessing to marry, but he'd always imagined he'd forgive Libby just as soon as she'd dumped him. For once, his own father's abandonment seemed almost tame.

But most of all he was appalled that he empathised with Libby whatsoever, when by definition empathy meant feeling on the same page as another person and she thought of him as a whole other book, on a different shelf altogether. The bottom shelf.

Rion put the glass down on the table with a bang. Well, maybe they would always be on different shelves in her eyes, but their bodies spoke the same language, and this time around he wasn't going to let her forget it. He was going to make her beg, and only then would he let her go.

Libby hadn't expected to turn on the light and find a room full of his photos and personal possessions, but it seemed fate had made up its mind to just keep dishing out the pain tonight.

Although she could have opened the door and asked him if she could sleep elsewhere, or gone and tried to find another room herself, the last thing she needed was to run into him and receive another insincere invitation to his bed.

Besides, she needed to train herself to look at his face and feel nothing, instead of remembering the man she'd fallen in love with. That man no longer existed. Her heart ached at the realisation, at the thought that her actions might be partly responsible—actions he couldn't or wouldn't understand. She wanted to believe there must have been some mistake, that he hadn't become a ruthless, blackmailing brute, that it was just a nightmare—but she knew it was the part before they'd met Spyros which had all been a dream.

So maybe finding herself in such close proximity to all his possessions was the best thing that could have happened. Maybe she could uncondition those old feelings and build up her resistance ready to confront the real thing again tomorrow? Like presenting images of a spider to an arachnophobe, she thought, remembering something she'd once read in an in-flight magazine about the way cognitive behavioural therapies worked.

But hadn't it also said something about the dangers of presenting the phobic with too much too quickly? She shook her head, wishing for the second time that day that she didn't recall everything in such categorical detail, before deciding that the analogy was pointless anyway. Because she wasn't *afraid* of Rion, she reasoned with herself, ignoring the voice which said *no, but you're afraid of the way he still makes you feel.*

But at least she had discovered the truth early—wouldn't have to go through the pain of slowly coming to realise that he only had space in his heart for money and power. And now she knew that making their separation official was one hundred per cent the right thing to be doing. That the way forward was to refuse to comply with his blackmail until he couldn't bear her remaining as his wife a moment longer. Yes, she was actually grateful for tonight, because it had banished all the doubts she'd started to have about whether getting divorced was the right thing to do. It was. Unequivocally.

At least she was sure she would feel that way once she'd slept on it.

CHAPTER SIX

LIBBY woke at six, after a surprisingly easy night's sleep. She put it down to emotional exhaustion, and the relief of having settled on a course of action. Six was actually relatively late by her standards; she'd been an early bird since her childhood, reading voraciously in the early hours of morning when her father wasn't around to forbid her on the grounds that no man wanted a wife more intelligent than he was. Now, getting up at the crack of dawn to lead an excursion, catch a flight, or meet a new tour group was part of her job description, and ordinarily she adored it.

So why did just the thought of returning to that life, even if she successfully got Rion to sign the divorce petition, fill her with such depression this morning? Because all these years she'd thought that if she saw him again she wouldn't feel anything any more, she supposed, and yesterday she'd realised she was wrong. Because he'd made her realise that the life she'd carved out for herself didn't make her as happy as she'd told herself it did. And because, just when she'd allowed herself to believe she had a shot at *real* happiness, she'd discovered the man who'd once made her so happy had been replaced by a man who wanted to control her for his own gain.

Well, today he was going to discover that she would not be controlled by anything or anyone, Libby thought defiantly, rifling through her suitcase and digging out a sleeveless top and skirt. She got up and pressed her ear to the door to see if she could hear any sounds of movement on the landing. Nothing. She was thankful that in giving her the co-ordinates of his bedroom, and having directed her to the bathroom to freshen up yesterday, he'd prevented her from having to embark on a Russian-Roulette-style door-opening session this morning, which would most certainly have resulted in waking him, and probably stumbling across him in bed too.

Appalled to catch herself lingering outside his door, wondering whether he still slept naked, Libby rushed to the bathroom and jumped straight in the shower. But she was frustrated to find jets of water shooting out from the walls to massage her body from every angle, and, despite the fact that she had to contend with different shower mechanisms all the time, she couldn't work out how to turn them off. Defeated, but adamant that she would not be subjected to such a sensual assault, she turned the temperature unarousingly low, soaped, rinsed, and then dried herself off briskly in record quick time before flinging on her clothes and leaving the house.

It was a gloriously sunny morning, with a light breeze rising off the ocean that caught the scent of wild thyme as it blew inland. To her relief, it blew her melancholy aside and immediately put her in the mood to explore.

She decided to turn right and begin in Metameikos's old town first, taking photos along the way and sketching out a rough map in her notebook. She told herself the old town was the most logical place to start, but if she was honest she was too curious about the place where he'd grown up not to start there. Especially when he'd always been so reluctant to talk about it, and tried to argue that there was nothing remotely sentimental about his decision to come back here. He'd admitted that he'd bought the house because as a child he'd sworn he'd own it one day, so surely there *was* more to his decision to come back to Metameikos than he was willing to reveal? After all, the place where you grew up always shaped the person you became, didn't it? Even if only in the sense that it made you want to escape it.

But as Libby began to wander through the streets she couldn't imagine Metameikos could have that effect on anyone, and knew almost instantly that it would go down well with the clientele who booked with Kate's Escapes. Yes, some parts were in need of serious rejuvenation, but at the same time she couldn't recall anywhere else she'd visited that was quite so charming: the rows of washing strung out across the narrow streets, the small gardens lovingly planted and teeming with butterflies, the natural stream of water that trickled down through the mountains to the village square, where locals gathered to collect water and exchange gossip.

But, she thought, stopping at a small café for a cup

of lemon tea and a delicious pastry, she didn't suppose stopping the rat race and enjoying life's simple pleasures would appeal to Rion. Yet he'd still chosen to return to that house—even though there were newer, far more luxurious and impressive properties that must have sprung up since his childhood.

So surely that meant he didn't want to escape the simple charm of the place where he'd grown up completely?

Or maybe it just conveniently happens to be the most politically neutral location in Metameikos, the voice of reason piped up in the back of her mind as she walked along the promenade towards the new town, the boats changing from small fishing vessels coming in from a morning's work to enormous yachts with last night's empty champagne bottles strewn across the deck, their curtains drawn tight. For if Metameikos did mean something else to him, then surely the few times he'd spoken about it he wouldn't have done so reluctantly. *And maybe he knows that having been raised here gives his bid for power an added credibility?* Yes, now she thought about it, it was obvious that that was the reason why he'd chosen to run for office in his home town—it increased his chances of winning. That, and the fact that, as Metameikos was the only independent province in Greece, if he *did* win his power would be far greater than if he'd simply become a member of the *vouli* in Athens. She cursed herself for wanting so desperately to believe she'd been mistaken about him when she knew it was so futile, and carried on.

After only half an hour of wandering between the

enormous, characterless, whitewashed villas that comprised the new town, Libby came to the decision that it was far too generic to warrant inclusion on any tour, and went back in the direction from which she'd come. She spent the rest of the morning in and out of a tiny museum that had been set up by a few of the locals who were keen to profit in a small way from the few tourists who ventured down the coast. The lady working there, who turned out to be a dear friend of Eurycleia's, was a mine of information, pointing out all the local sites of historical interest and keenly offering ideas when Libby suggested she might be interested in securing accommodation for small groups.

After taking lunch at the taverna across the street, where she sampled some delicious sea bream that had been caught by the local fishermen that morning, Libby decided to head back to the house, filled with enthusiasm for plotting out a potential itinerary based on what she'd discovered so far. Until she passed the amphitheatre, and was reminded that running any such tour would involve being virtually on his doorstep. It made her stomach roll so unpleasantly that she was almost tempted to report back to Kate that the whole of Metameikos was unsuitable for tours.

But that feeling will pass once you're divorced— once you've forced him to regret trying to control you like this, she reassured herself as she reached the house and let herself in through the back door, ignoring the army of doubts that sprang up in response.

'Where have you been?' He was hunched forward on

a stool at the breakfast bar when she entered the kitchen, eating bruschetta with one hand whilst tapping away on his laptop with the other, but he stopped both and fixed condemning eyes on her the second she entered.

'Oh, you know—here and there,' she said waspishly, wanting to feel glad that his anger meant she'd success-fully pushed him one step closer to signing the divorce papers, but feeling the opposite.

'You don't think I deserve to know your whereabouts?'

'You haven't cared about my whereabouts for the last five years.'

'Things are different now.'

No, they weren't. He hadn't suddenly started caring. All he meant was that now where she was and what she did reflected on him. 'Perhaps you should have checked that I agree with you on that.'

'I rather thought a basic code of conduct was implicit.'

'Did you?' she said scathingly, sucking air between her teeth and tapping her forefinger against her chin. 'Oh, dear. So you mean that you were gambling on my code of conduct coinciding with yours? I really think we ought to have compared notes first. But if we must do it retrospectively, let's see… There was that gorgeous young waiter this morning, and I just presumed that it was okay to—'

'Don't play games with me, Libby,' he growled, in-stantly reaching out his hand to encircle her wrist.

The sheer eroticism of his thumb on her pulse-point made her bravado falter. 'I only popped out to do some research for work.'

The tension in Rion's shoulders eased marginally. When he'd woken up and found her gone he'd thought—he didn't know what he'd thought. That she'd left him again, he supposed, or that she was out making plans to. 'Then perhaps if you're going to be *popping out* in future it would be courteous if you could let me know where you're going—or at the very least how I can contact you if I needed to find out.'

'You're asking me for my phone number?'

'Do you usually reserve it for men you're not married to?'

Libby was ready with a curt response and a fake number, but his words stopped her in her tracks. No, she didn't usually give out her number full-stop, because she didn't like the thought of anyone keeping tabs on her the way her parents always had. But for the first time ever Libby suddenly considered how sad that was. Yes, in the intervening years she had achieved the independence she'd always craved, but the result was that no one ever knew where she was going unless it was detailed in an itinerary. And, whilst there was a sense of freedom in that, it also screamed loneliness. If she went missing, who would notice? A tour group of people she'd never met before?

'Okay,' she mumbled. 'Seems reasonable.'

As he whipped out his mobile and she began to list the digits, Libby tried not to think about the *we're each other's next of kin,* but *we don't even know each other's phone numbers* argument she'd levelled at him as a reason why they should get a divorce two days ago. If she did, she'd be forced to admit that, even though she had every reason to be certain that excluding him from her life completely was the right thing to do, she seemed to be encouraging him to waltz back into it.

When he'd finished punching in her number he swiftly replaced his phone in his pocket, took his plate to the draining board and shut down his laptop.

'I have a meeting this afternoon,' he said, flicking a glance at his watch. 'I'll be back around five.'

'Oh? What kind of meeting?'

The corner of his mouth lifted in amusement as he slid on his dark suit jacket and ran a hand down his tie— far, far too sexily. 'For someone who considers it an intrusion for her husband to question *her* whereabouts, you have an awful lot of interest.' He raised one eyebrow provocatively.

'I'm just a little surprised. I presumed you'd demand my presence at every event even remotely connected to your campaign.'

'Well, you'll be pleased to know that, save for the Mayor's pre-election party next week, I don't require you to do anything other than remain here, gracing the marital home.' He nodded to the sun terrace, slipped on his shoes and opened the front door. 'I dare say you won't find it too much of a hardship. See you later.'

In a moment of impulsive anger, Libby grabbed one of Eurycleia's biscuits from the plate on the side and threw it after him, but he shut the door so quickly behind himself that it didn't connect with anything other than the wood, breaking into a trillion pieces and falling in a shower of crumbs to the floor.

So, she thought acrimoniously as she stomped over to sweep up the mess, full of guilt that Eurycleia's baking had taken the brunt of her anger, not only was he using her, but he'd become a blatant misogynist as well. He didn't want a woman with a brain who might actually aid his campaign. He just wanted a walking, talking cliché. No wonder he'd sent Eurycleia away— after all, why did he need a housekeeper when he had a wife 'gracing the marital home'?

Well, she thought, her eyes scanning the kitchen and finding his laptop, if this morning hadn't convinced him that she wasn't prepared to play any such role, then this afternoon would. Quickly she turned it on and ran a search for 'public meeting, Orion Delikaris, Metameikos'. The results immediately threw up the details of the town hall she'd passed that morning, and a start time of two-thirty. Perfect.

It was two thirty-three when Libby turned the corner of the street and saw Rion's Bugatti parked outside the town hall. Which was pretty good going, considering she'd only left the house at ten past, and had been on foot during the hottest part of the day. She pinched her top at the neck and fanned it to create a cool column of air down her body, took a moment to catch her breath, then stepped inside.

The hall was filled with a large cross-section of people. There were fishermen who must have finished the early-morning trawl and come up from the docks, elderly men with backgammon boards tucked under their arms, women with babies strapped to their chests, and a group of students she presumed must be from the somewhat dilapidated college she'd spotted on the other side of the old town that morning. Perceptive, Libby thought as more people filed in behind her, to choose the time just before siesta, when everyone was walking past on their way home.

'Welcome, and thank you for coming.'

Libby heard his voice at the front of the room and stood up on tiptoes, trying to find a gap between the heads.

'The aim of this meeting is to explain the main improvements we plan to make to Metameikos if we're successful in the forthcoming elections. However, first and foremost, we want this afternoon to be a no-holds-barred opportunity for you to ask questions of us.'

There was a murmur of surprise from the crowd, as if such an invitation was unheard of, but, as Libby finally found a direct eyeline to the low stage, she was almost too mesmerised to notice. Because all of a sudden she realised that her husband was the embodiment of the phrase 'natural-born leader'. She'd never really thought of him that way before, but now he was up there he looked so commanding, so confident and so capable, that even *she* felt an instinctive need to follow him.

She silenced her inner floozy, which whispered, *Yes, straight to bed.* Because, whilst she couldn't go on pretending that she wasn't attracted to him, when had she ever been turned on by what boiled down to a display of power, arrogance and control? Since it was accompanied by a look which said he was willing to do anything for the good of these people, she supposed. But then *looking* that way was what politicians were best at, wasn't it?

'I didn't realise you were coming,' a voice behind her whispered, suddenly interrupting her thoughts. She turned to see a stylishly dressed young man, hand out-stretched. 'I'm Stephanos, one of Rion's press officers.'

Libby shook his hand warily, wondering how on earth he knew who she was.

'You were snapped together outside the theatre last night,' he said, reading her puzzled expression. 'It made the front page of the *Metameikos Tribune* this morning.'

Libby sighed. 'Then I guess today is a good day for you.'

He raised his eyebrows towards the stage. 'It has the potential to get even better. Come with me?'

For a ridiculous moment she wondered whether Rion had spotted her in the crowd and sent him down to get her. Until it occurred to her that not only was it unfea-sible that he'd seen her, or had the chance to do anything about it, but that if he had he probably would have dis-patched someone to send her home.

Stephanos had obviously just noticed her and recog-nised an opportunity to make use of her. And, although part of the reason why she was here was to protest against being used, the opportunity to defy Rion's in-structions and prove that his colleague clearly didn't share his chauvinistic opinion that she should be 'gracing the marital home' was too tempting to resist.

She nodded. 'Sure.'

Stephanos led her to the side of the crowd and along

the edge of the room, whilst Rion launched into an explanation of his plans for a new hospital. His speech
was flawless—or at least it was until they were a few
metres away from the stage, when she heard him
hesitate mid-sentence.

Libby knew instantly that their movements had caught
his attention. She raised her head, and was met by a look
of horrified disapproval which momentarily rooted her
to the spot. But then, just as quickly, he looked away and
continued speaking, his composure seemingly unaffected
after all. Blinking to check she hadn't imagined it, Libby
saw that Stephanos had forged ahead and was beckoning
for her to follow him up some discreet steps at the edge
of the stage. Still dazed, she caught up with him at the
top, where he quickly grabbed an extra chair out of
nowhere, added it the semi-circle of people seated behind
Rion, and signalled for her to join them.

As Rion began the second half of his speech he
sensed her sit down behind him, and felt the tendrils of
dread begin to snake around his heart. He'd worked so
hard for this: the one remaining goal he was yet to fulfil.
Now, thanks to his fixation on proving to her that he had
become a success, that she was still as hot for him as he
was for her, she was about to condemn him to failure. To
lose him the one chance he had to put right everything
that was still so wrong here. How foolish he'd been to
suppose that two weeks of luxury and a shot at what she
wanted would be enough to keep her mouth shut. Now
he thought about it, it was obvious; of *course* she'd seize
the opportunity to ruin him. The prospect of a man like

him holding any position of power was bound to appall her.

Rion gritted his teeth, praying he could transmit a telepathic command to Stephanos to get her off the stage. *Now.* He understood why he'd brought her up here: since she'd turned up of her own accord it would avoid any negative speculation as to why she was in the crowd and not by his side. But what Stephanos didn't realise was that they'd have more than just speculation to worry about if someone directed a question at her or if she decided to open her mouth.

But Rion, it seemed, was not capable of telepathy, because, whilst he could see Stephanos at the very edge of the stage, the only movement he was making was with his mouth, silently repeating *Start the questions.*

Reluctantly, Rion wrapped up his explanation of how the affordable housing scheme would work. 'So now it's over to you. Who has a question for me?'

'Or for one of us,' his recently demoted campaign manager, who'd always been keen to push the team approach, chipped in.

Rion pasted on a smile which didn't reach his eyes. 'Of course—or for the team.'

'I have a question.' A middle-aged man at the front of the crowd raised his hand, and Rion signalled for him to go on. 'You say there'll be a new hospital, and five hundred new houses that the likes of us'll be able to afford, but after that how do we know that the rest of Metameikos won't become like it is up there?' He motioned in the general direction of the new town amidst murmurs of agreement.

'How *indeed*?' another male voice—sly and deeply unpleasant—piped up from further back in the crowd.

Libby leaned slightly to the right and saw immediately that the owner of the voice was the grubby-looking man who had been standing with Spyros and his wife last night.

'For wasn't Delikaris Experiences' last project an exclusive block of apartments?'

There were renewed mutterings from the crowd, this time of concern.

'Indeed it was,' Rion said with calm assurance. 'And, whilst I consider my business endeavours entirely separate from what I hope to achieve in Metameikos, since you have asked I will gladly explain why that was.'

Spyros's man looked triumphant, but only for a second. Rion continued. 'Athens is the best location from which to run Delikaris Experiences. A capital city is always best for business, and,' he said with a proud curl of his lips, 'why would I choose anywhere other than the capital of *Greece*? However, it's also a very expensive place to live. In order that I might help my employees I bought a block of apartments which had fallen into disrepair and had the whole building renovated— far more cheaply than if each apartment had been bought and refurbished individually. It allowed me to offer them to my staff to buy or to rent at a very reasonable price, if they so chose.'

Spyros's man looked incensed that his question had backfired—until he seized upon a counter-argument. 'Because you do not pay your staff enough for them to be able to afford a home on the open market, Mr Delikaris?'

'No, Stamos, because I believe people deserve a break. So to answer your question, sir—' he returned his attention to the man at the front '—I believe luxury has its place, but I'm no fonder of the idea of Metameikos becoming a sea of over-priced holiday homes than you are. Once I've built five hundred affordable homes, I promise you I will endeavour to build five hundred more. After all, I'm sure your children would like to be able to buy homes of their own one day too.'

The man nodded earnestly, and the murmurs of the crowd became more approving, until Stamos interrupted once again.

'Oh, yes, we learned yesterday that, contrary to wide-spread opinion, you're the ultimate family man. This is your wife, is it not?' He pointed at Libby.

There was no gasp of surprise. It seemed the news had travelled fast. Instead there was a sea of awkward yet curious glances, as though Stamos had asked an in-appropriate question, but one to which everyone wanted to know the answer.

She took a deep breath, wishing she could see the ex-pression on Rion's face instead of the back of his head. But the composure in his voice suggested it would be giving no more away than it ever did.

'Indeed. My wife and I have been apart for some time, but I'm delighted to say that's no longer the case.' He turned to look at her fleetingly, before nodding as if to invite more questions. Preferably *not* about the woman he hadn't wanted at this meeting in the first place, she thought glibly.

'And was it your husband's heart-warming policies that drew you back to him just in time for his election campaign?' Stamos said archly, directing his question at her.

Rion's head turned sharply towards the edge of the stage, anger flaring in his eyes, but Stephanos shot him a warning look which said *It will do more harm than good if we throw him out.* When he turned to face the front again he saw to his horror that Libby had stepped forward to take the microphone.

'No,' she said, and heard him draw in a sharp breath behind her.

It was tempting to blurt out the truth, but the thought of it made her lungs fill with the guilt that had been rising ever since last night. And suddenly she wondered whether if she bit her tongue at this moment, when she had the chance to ruin him, he might see that she was sorry for the pain she had caused him, whether it might make him reconsider whether she really deserved to be used in this way.

'No. Actually, I wasn't aware of my husband's decision to run in this election until…very recently. It was my career which led me back to Athens, where we were reunited.'

'But you are undoubtedly in full support of your husband's policies now?'

'From what I have just heard, yes.' She paused, drawing the line at actually lying. They *did* sound good, but so did a lot of things which came out of his mouth. 'But they are as new to me as I am sure they are to many of you. So, since I'm afraid I have never believed in adopting the opinions of those close to me simply because of the ties of marriage or blood, ask me again when I have had time to mull over the facts.'

To Libby's surprise the whole room suddenly filled with delighted applause—from the women in the crowd, who seemed to be bowled over that she had spoken her mind, and from the men, who nudged each other knowingly, as if it was heartening to know that even Orion Delikaris had a headstrong wife to contend with. From everyone except Stamos, who slipped out of the back door with a face like thunder.

Libby resumed her seat as new questions about healthcare and schooling began to pour in thick and fast, the crowd's tongues apparently loosened by the moment.

'You're a genius,' Stephanos whispered from the edge of the stage.

But something about the look on Rion's face told her that was not going to be an opinion he shared.

CHAPTER SEVEN

AS LIBBY sank down into the low leather seat of the Bugatti, Rion removed his tie, loosened his collar, and turned the key in the ignition. The car roared into life.

He had maintained his flawless composure during the remainder of the meeting, effortlessly answering each new question from the floor with just the right blend of consideration, substance and wit, but she'd known that inwardly he was seething. And if she'd been in any doubt, then the firm hand at her back and his frosty silence as he'd escorted her to the car afterwards had made it explicitly clear.

Well, Libby was positively seething herself. Yes, she'd gone to the meeting with the intention of riling him, but surely he could see that in the end she'd decided to try and breed a little common decency? It seemed she'd made a serious error of judgement. He didn't have an ounce of common decency left.

'Has it escaped your notice that I actually did you a favour in there?' she shot out suddenly, convinced that if she didn't say something then the car's windows would implode under the tension, 'That the people of Metameikos got to see you as a human being instead of a billionaire who flies around the sky in his own plane and whirls around the streets in his Bugatti?' She made a disparaging spinning gesture with her forefinger.

'Hark at you, "Lady" Ashworth, lecturing *me* about keeping in touch with the common people.'

'I'm not the one swanning around in the fancy transport.'

'No, you're the one who—in the absence of your parents' wealth to wallow in—has come to wallow in mine.'

She seethed at the accusation. 'Being forced to do so has only reminded me that money counts for nothing. Doesn't it occur to you that the people of Metameikos might feel the same?'

Rion's knuckles went white against the steering wheel, and for a moment his fury was so acute he couldn't speak. 'You think that money *counts for nothing*? Here, of all places? But of course—why *would* you think anything else when you've never known what it is to have none?'

'That's not what I meant. Just because my parents have money it doesn't mean I have no idea—'

'How it feels to live in squalor? Oh, yes, I'm forgetting the slum of an apartment *I* made you live in.'

She shook her head, wondering how it was possible that he always got her so wrong.

'Just because my parents have money it doesn't mean I have no idea about poverty, Rion. I've been all over the world—*all* over it, not just to the places with bright city lights.'

'And what did you do when you saw it? Put away your digital camera and thank God you were born lucky?'

'I did what I could,' she said solemnly, turning to look out of the window. Which hadn't been much when she'd been living on her wits herself. But the fund at Kate's Escape she'd set up, to encourage staff and clients to donate to the areas they visited which were most in need, was now really starting to make a difference.

'What I meant…' She took a deep breath, steering her thoughts back to their original argument as they approached the house. 'What I meant is that I doubt your display of excess is doing anything to endear you to your electorate.'

'You don't think so?' He raised his eyebrows patronisingly. 'Surely I don't need to remind you that I was a boy in that crowd once?'

'No, you don't need to remind me.' That was why they were here, instead of in Athens or anywhere else. He wanted power to go with his wealth and success, and the added authenticity of doing it here gave him the best chance of getting it. She missed his grimace.

'Then—tricky as this may be for you—try for a moment to think yourself into the mindset of someone living in the old town. Wouldn't you be inspired to see a man who started in the same place as you are now returning home a success?'

Libby thought about it, and about the announcement that he intended to plough his own wealth into hospitals and houses too. She had to admit that if she didn't know he was only in this for the power and the thrill of winning then she probably would. In fact, she didn't know why for a minute she'd supposed the people would think anything else; he'd painstakingly considered *every* aspect of his image and made sure it was tailored towards gaining maximum support, hadn't he? That was why she was here. But what was wrong with showing people that he was a human being as well as a success story?

'So, if you're so keen for the people of Metameikos to feel an affinity with you, how can you possibly be angry about what happened back there?'

Rion pulled onto the driveway and killed the engine. How could he be angry about what happened back there? Oh, there were of plenty of ways: he could be angry that he'd allowed his desire for her to weaken his faculties; that for a moment she of all people had held his fate in her hands whilst he'd looked on powerlessly; that he hadn't even slaked his goddamned desire for her yet!

He flung open the car door. 'I am needed in a conference call with Delikaris headquarters.' He looked down at his watch. 'Now.'

Libby scrambled after him as he unlocked the front door, desperate to force him to see how unreasonable he was being. 'If you can't think of an answer then why not consider the fact that maybe there isn't a reason? I could have told everyone exactly how you're capitalising on my return, but I chose to help you, and yet you still look like you're about to explode.'

The second the words were out of her mouth Rion turned so sharply back on himself that she almost crashed straight into him. 'You're right,' he breathed, stretching out his arm and pushing the front door shut behind her head. For a second she froze, her eyes wide with hope that he was about to announce that he'd been wrong to try and use her in this way, to reveal that he was still the old Rion she'd fallen in love with. But then he continued. 'I *am* about to explode. And so are you.' He reached down for her hand and then raised it to his chest, placing it at the exact point where the fabric of his shirt gave way to flesh.

It was so unexpected that for a second she just stood there, feeling the heat of his hair-roughened chest, the pounding of his heart which began to reverberate through her body so she couldn't tell which was her rhythm and which was his, almost as if they were—

'No!' she gasped, wrenching her hand away and drawing in a fast, deep breath, hoping the rush of oxygen would kick her brain into gear, remind her that he didn't really want her, that he wasn't the same man any more, that it would only lead to heartache. She tried to take a step backwards, but she was already up against the front door, and when she took a side-step to the right he mirrored it, keeping her hemmed in.

'No?' he said huskily. 'That *isn't* what you want? Then why is your body temperature soaring? And why tear your hand away as though you're terrified of what you might do next?'

'I'm not terrified—'

'Good—then there's no reason to remove it, is there?' He reached for her hand again and placed it back inside his shirt, his eyes never leaving hers.

Libby's breath caught in her throat. So now she was damned if she removed her hand and damned if she didn't? She lowered her eyes, desperate to reduce the effect that touching him was having on her by blocking out the sight of him, knowing her only hope was to try and convince him she felt nothing whatsoever.

Gently he ran his forefinger along her outstretched right arm and softly up her neck. Libby closed her eyes and shook her head, so that the short length of her hair fell forwards. For the first time since she'd had it cut, in a bid to start afresh upon arriving in Manchester five years ago, she wished she hadn't—just so she had something more substantial to hide behind.

'Don't you know that trying to look away says even more than if you just drank me in with your eyes, as I know you're longing to do?' he murmured. 'Do you think I don't remember how you always hid behind your hair…' he smoothed the wisps away from her face now, tucking them behind her ear in a gesture which made Libby's stomach lurch in painful remembrance '…when you wanted me most?'

She opened her eyes wide and looked directly into the depths of his, hoping he didn't notice the increased pressure of her hand against his chest as she fought to steady herself. 'The meaning of things can change, Rion. Just because I lacked self-confidence then it does not mean I avert my gaze out of coyness now.'

'Coyness?' He laughed nastily. 'No, I'm well aware that's not the reason.'

Wounded at his insinuation, Libby dropped her lashes again. 'Then why can't you just accept that I don't want to look at you or to…touch you?' She removed her hand from his chest a second time, and stared down at her palm as if it had betrayed her.

'I don't know,' he answered, marching his fingertips against his lower lip in feigned deliberation. 'Maybe it's because you can't say that and look me in the eye. Maybe it's because ever since you turned up in my office you've been looking at me the way a man who is starving might look at a banquet. So why don't you just come and taste it?'

She heard her breathing grow heavy, felt the exaggerated rise and fall of her chest. Why had she bothered even *trying* to fool him? He could read the subtle body language of people he'd only just met, for goodness' sake, never mind the unsubtleties of hers.

And he's been using that against you from the start, a voice reminded her from deep within the lust-filled labyrinth of her mind. *Not because he desires you, but for the benefit of his political career.*

Which meant that if she looked hard enough she'd catch the look of reluctance in his eyes, she thought with both pain and relief. For surely if she could *see* that his desire was nothing but a mask he wore, as a means to an end, she'd have the strength and the self-respect to walk away?

But as she flicked her eyes up to his face again there

wasn't even a hint of disinclination. And although it had been missing yesterday too, then she'd been sure that he'd just been turned on by the challenge of proving he was better than her 'other man'. Now he knew that there was no other man. So could it really be possible that... *she* was turning him on?

'Stuck for an answer yourself now, *gineka mou*?'

'No, I'm—'

'Still here,' he finished, stepping back and sweeping his arm across the gap between them, to emphasise the fact that he was no longer blocking her escape.

'Yes,' she whispered, willing the words *I'm just leaving* to come out of her mouth. But they didn't. Because how could she leave when he was looking at her the way he had that very first day when she'd walked into her father's showroom, as if no amount of her would ever be enough?

'Yes,' she repeated, 'I'm still here, and I...don't want to go anywhere.'

Triumph and arousal surged through Rion's veins. He'd never been in any doubt that her body craved this as much as his did, but for a minute there he'd wondered whether the shame she felt at that was going to win out all over again. But it hadn't, and that made *him* the winner. Because this time around there would be no holding back.

'Good,' he growled, lowering his head. 'Because right here is perfect with me.'

Libby's stomach did a part-fearful, part-excited somersault as she realised he'd interpreted her words literally. He'd made it clear that he suspected she'd had other lovers, and thanks to her failure to correct him he probably presumed that she was now some experienced seductress who was used to making love in the middle of the day, wherever the urge took her. And if that was the kind of woman he was used to making love to, she was bound to disappoint him.

An arrow of pain shot through her at the thought, but as his mouth descended to feast on hers with such hot, hedonistic pleasure that she wouldn't have been surprised if she'd actually caught alight, her fears didn't just diminish, they were eclipsed by sensation completely.

Of course he'd always known exactly how to turn her on—he'd *introduced* her to the pleasures her own body was capable of—but he'd always rebuffed her attempts to learn what turned *him* on. She'd always supposed it was because once he'd taken her to bed she hadn't excited him half as much as he'd expected, but now he was showing her that just exploring her mouth was driving him wild, and, to Libby, that was the most powerful aphrodisiac she'd ever experienced.

Desperate to learn what else he liked, she used his earlier action as a guide and hurriedly unbuttoned his shirt. He sucked in a deliciously impatient breath as she encouraged it over his shoulders and began to explore the hard planes of his chest, skimming her fingers over the sensitive area of his nipple without restriction.

In the next instant he returned the favour, his fingers moving quickly to the buttons of her top. But rather than discarding it immediately he placed his hands flat against her tummy and slowly began to move them upwards beneath the thin fabric.

Libby closed her eyes and arched her back against the wall, imagining the symmetrical pattern his hands were making on her body as they skimmed upwards until they reached her bra, where they changed shape in order to cup her breasts. It sent a dart of need between her legs so acute that it was painful.

'Rion!'

Aroused, but frustrated by the material obstructions, she scrambled to discard both offending items herself. She rid herself of her top, but as it hit the floor his hands came behind her to work the fastening of her bra. Slowly he peeled it away from her body. Like a gift to be unwrapped, she thought glowingly, *and enjoyed.* Because, whilst he clearly hadn't forgotten the way she liked to be touched, now he was revelling in the way *he* liked to touch her, stroking, kneading, tasting.

Libby groaned, and he smiled in delight, his hands going in search of more pleasure, trailing lower, finding the globes of her bottom beneath her skirt, reaching for the hook, the zip. She kicked off her sandals, the marble floor cold beneath her feet, and in seconds she was completely naked before him.

Desperate for him to join her, she began to feather kisses down his chest whilst her hands moved to unbutton his trousers. He moaned in encouragement, but it excited her so much that her fingers lost their way.

He came to her aid, discarding the rest of his clothes at speed—only stopping to slip his leather wallet out of his trouser pocket before they hit the ground. But Libby didn't even notice. She was too transfixed by the smooth beauty of his erection.

She'd had the instinctive desire to touch him in all his glory since the very first time she'd seen him naked, but in the past he'd always steered her hand away. Now, encouraged by his pleasure at her exploration of his chest, she pushed those memories aside and took his tip between her fingers, running her thumb around its head.

She felt his whole body go still, his breathing become loud and fast and irregular. She looked up, excitement rippling through her at the effect she was having on him. His eyes were wide and black with desire. She moved her hand to stroke the whole length of him. His eyes grew darker still. This time he did not stop her.

At least not until it was obvious to both of them that unless she stopped now, this was going to be over too soon.

Instantly he turned his attention back to his wallet. He'd already torn open the silver foil before it occurred to Libby that his protecting himself was actually unnecessary, given that she was on the pill. She'd only gone on it for the convenience of knowing when to expect her previously irregular periods whilst travelling, had never had reason to consider its other function before. But she sensed it would rather shatter the mood if she suddenly tried to explain that now, when his hands were already sweeping purposefully up thighs, beneath her bottom...

Deftly, his upper body taut with strength, Rion lifted her up and took a step forward, so that her back was supported by the wall. Libby gasped at the sheer eroticism of what his body was proposing, but as she wrapped her legs around his waist, her body accepted it instinctively.

The feeling as he drove into her was exquisite. Maybe it was sinful, a crime against her sex to be glad that he'd made no attempt to tenderly touch her, to check that she was ready for him first. But to her it was proof that they'd never been closer. That he understood he could toss the rulebook out of the window because she couldn't wait a moment longer. Any more than he could.

His thrusts were urgent, primitive, perfect. She looked down at his thick dark hair, ran her hands through it, over the hard muscles of his arms that held her there so effortlessly, loving the incongruent looks of both power and powerlessness she saw intermittently on his face, heard in the shameless, guttural sounds that he mouthed into the hollow of her shoulder.

She leaned her head against the wall, the movement arching her back so that she could feel her nipples graze the taut plane of his chest. Every nerve-ending in her body was tight—no, loose—no, a whole mixture of sensations. As if her body had given up trying to work out which ones it was supposed to be possible to feel at the same time and was just making her feel *everything*.

'Oh!'

Her internal muscles began to contract around his hardness, but she wanted him to go first. Taking a risk that she could hold on, she wrapped her legs around his back even more tightly and drew him in deeper.

It was a risk worth taking, because at the exact

moment that her muscles clamped around him totally she felt Rion give one final, colossal thrust and cry out his own release.

And for one single moment there was just stillness. Perfect, silent stillness, accompanied by the most unexpected feeling of liberation.

Until he spoke.

'Now do you see that we're driven by exactly the same urges, *gineka mou*?' he drawled, depositing her back down on the cold marble floor, the look of unwavering power back on his face.

But Libby was not about to forget that only moments before it had been none so steady.

'No,' she said boldly, 'now I see that my defiance actually turns you on.'

CHAPTER EIGHT

'Your defiance?' Rion's mouth twitched in amusement.

It had occurred to her the second she'd seen that look of powerlessness on his face. He'd said he wanted her to simply remain in the marital home, implied that all he needed was any woman to play the role of his wife for the duration of his campaign, but when she'd defied him, showed him the kind of independent woman she'd become, it had turned him on. He'd made love to her like never before, as though deep down maybe he *did* want something from life that had nothing to do with this election, with power or success. And it felt as if she might have just seen the first glimmer of light at the end of a black, black tunnel.

'You don't think it a little coincidental that your desire just happened to arise at the exact moment I made it clear that I will not allow you to control me?'

He gave a loud, disparaging laugh. 'No, *gineka mou*. I think it was just a question of how long you could go on fighting it.'

'So making love to me right then was all part of your

nicely controlled plan, was it? I don't think so, Rion. I disobeyed you, and even though it frustrated the hell out of you, it aroused you so much…' She hesitated, still having to remind herself it was true. The sight of his manhood still standing proud just a few feet away from her helped. 'It aroused you so much that you even missed your precious conference call.'

He flicked a glance at his watch. 'So I did.' He shrugged nonchalantly. 'But I dare say it will do no harm if word gets about that I missed it because I was busy devoting time to my wife.'

Libby bit down so hard on her lower lip that she could taste blood. So, even though their lovemaking was the one thing which hadn't had anything to do with his campaign, he was still going to use it for that purpose rather than admit otherwise.

Furiously she swiped her skirt and top from the floor and wrenched them on. 'Well, if that was really what this was all about, why didn't you say? We could have gone to your office and set up the webcam, so your colleagues could have photographic evidence of just how attentive you are.'

Rion's mouth twisted in disgust. 'Don't be depraved.'

'No? You think you prefer it when I'm the submissive little wife, do you? Fine, let's see.'

She could have done better given half an hour in a charity shop, but fifteen minutes later, as Libby heard him descend the stairs, she was pretty sure she would have the desired effect. On her lower half she was wearing a faded old ankle-length skirt—the one she always kept in the bottom of her suitcase for slipping over her shorts in case an excursion involved going inside a temple or a church where it was necessary to cover her legs—and on her top half she had a brown and orange paisley tunic, which looked quite funky when she wore it with a belt and boots, but was an absolute fashion disaster with the long skirt. Coupled with Eurycleia's apron, and a strategic splattering of flour on her face, she was pretty sure she had un-sexy subservience written all over her.

He was talking rapidly in Greek when he entered the living room, head down, phone pressed to his ear. Libby translated. He was apologising for missing the conference call. Quickly she put down the rolling pin she'd just extracted from one of the kitchen drawers and strained to hear whether he really did have the nerve to cite quality time with her as his excuse.

But just as she was about to find out the rolling pin slid off the edge of the surface and hit the marble floor with an almighty crash.

Rion's eyes flew to her instantly, and she abandoned the curse that had been on her lips, morphing it into a polite, whispered apology, which she swiftly replaced with the blithe smile she'd made up her mind to keep plastered to her face for as long as it took her to discover whether that really had been a glimmer of light at the end of the tunnel, or just a mirage.

He looked her up and down as if she was insane, swiftly moved in the opposite direction so that she couldn't hear a damned thing he was saying, and only turned round to face her again once he'd cut the call.

'What the hell are you doing?'

Libby eased the honey off the spoon and into the mixing bowl with her finger. 'Oh, you know, the biscuits Eurycleia made were running low, so I thought I'd better make us some more.' She pretended to scrutinise the recipe she'd found. 'How about you? Off out?'

Rion looked down at his fresh white shirt and nodded warily, as if he needed to be careful about what details he gave away in case she followed him again. 'I have an evening meeting with my team.'

'Well, good luck,' she said, suppressing the urge to vomit at her own sickly-sweet tone. 'I'll still be here when you get home, just the way you like it.'

'Not *exactly* the way I like it,' he drawled.

'No?' she asked hopefully.

'No,' he breathed, and suddenly he came up behind her, removed her right hand from the mixing bowl, placed her finger in his mouth and then slowly began to suck off the honey. 'I'd prefer it a little more like this.'

Libby's whole body was still on fire ten minutes later, long after he'd returned her hand to the bowl with a lingering look and left for his meeting. She shook her head and began stirring the biscuit mixture far more violently than was necessary. This was going to take time, that was all. It was overly optimistic to suppose that the results would be instantaneous if she just acted a little domesticated and looked as if she'd got dressed in the dark. But she had no doubt that he'd soon cease to show any interest in her whatsoever, and be forced to admit that her defiance alone turned him on.

And then declare that he didn't want her acting as a caricature of his wife, but to be his wife for real? *Oh, don't be ridiculous, Libby,* she remonstrated as she dropped the biscuit rounds haphazardly onto a baking sheet. The best she could hope for was that he'd realise that blackmailing her wasn't worth the effort, and just sign the divorce papers.

But as she closed the door of the oven, leaned her back against its warmth and remembered the limitless joy she'd felt back in his arms, she couldn't stop herself from hoping.

In the days which followed, almost all of Rion's time was taken up with the campaign. When he wasn't attending meetings, or trawling the rest of the province to drum up support, he was on the phone to Delikaris headquarters, checking everything was running smoothly in his absence.

It gave Libby the perfect opportunity play the bland wife to the letter. She didn't ask too many questions, nor express too many opinions. She didn't attempt to accompany him anywhere, and although she quietly continued with her work during the day, she always made sure she was home before he was. She left the fridge well-stocked, the house clean and tidy, and continued to wear the drabbest clothes she could find.

And it worked.

Over a week had now passed, and Rion had not made love to her again.

Yes, on the rare occasions that they'd found themselves in the same room he'd still looked at her as though he wanted to lick honey off more than her finger, but she put it down to a half-hearted effort to continue with the pretence that she was wrong. Admittedly, the ultimate test would have been her waiting in his bed every night, rather than opting for the room next door— out of fear that she wouldn't be able to help *herself*— but she'd always passed off her decision as the action of a considerate wife who knew her busy husband needed uninterrupted sleep, whilst leaving her door ajar should he wish to prove her wrong.

But he hadn't. Not once. So, whilst he hadn't yet admitted that she actually left him cold this way, she remained certain that it would only be a matter of time before he did. And, God, she prayed it would be sooner rather than later.

Because acting this way all the time made her feel as if her wings had been clipped, she justified quickly, *not* because she was yearning for a repeat performance of that afternoon. Except, to her surprise, she didn't *actually* feel as if her wings had been clipped at all. Even though he was out almost as frequently as he had been in the early days of their marriage, it didn't bother her in the same way that it had done before she'd had her own focus in her work. In fact, she actually quite enjoyed the domesticity, the being in one place rather than finding herself in a different hotel room every night.

In short, her time here had proved that in the last five years she had successfully taken control of her life to such a degree that she did now feel properly ready to share her life with someone, and she wanted to. Which, she decided, might have just knocked her father naming her Liberty off the top spot of the list of greatest ironies of her life. Because, aside from some amazing sex, everything pointed to the fact that the only thing her husband wanted was world domination.

She drew in a deep breath, the memory of his lovemaking scorching across her mind *again*. She needed a distraction. It was too late to go back to work on another potential itinerary, Rion would be home soon, and cleaning would be pointless—the house was already spotless. She looked out of the window. The garden it was, then.

So she was still playing at it, Rion thought as he stepped out of the back door and spotted her picking figs from the tree behind the old swing seat. For a minute there he thought she'd gone out, given up this ridiculous pretence.

Didn't she know he was hot for her whatever she did? If she wanted to try and repel him she could at least try something a bit more drastic, like listing every one of their wedding vows she'd broken. Not that it would have had any greater effect, he thought grimly as he watched her reach up, the loose-fitting top she'd no doubt purposely chosen for its modesty paradoxically exposing her flat stomach, making him hard.

But it wasn't *his* desire she was really trying to deny, was it? Rion clenched his teeth, frustrated that she'd managed to convince herself that it was for so long. If it went on much longer—even though he'd sworn to himself that he'd wait for her to come to him—he might just have to show her it wasn't. His body—no, *her* body—was driving him too damned crazy.

And that frustrated him even more. He was supposed to be taking pleasure in wreaking his revenge, preparing to let her go with her desire half but never fully satiated. But the truth was that intention was slowly slinking away, because he didn't want to let her go. Coming home to her felt too good, and he was beginning to wonder whether her wistful looks meant she was beginning to feel the same way. He gritted his teeth. No, he knew that was impossible, that it was probably just a plot to win his sympathy, get him to sign sooner or something. Was he forgetting what he'd promised himself? He would never be so gullible again.

'Ripe?' he said huskily, coming up behind her.

Libby jumped and let go of the branch, which sprang back, creating a shower of purple which dropped to the floor and exploded red around their feet.

'I didn't hear you get back,' she said, almost crossly, then checked herself and sweetened her tone. 'Yes, they're ripe. Would you like one?'

'Tempting, but it will keep for now,' he drawled. 'I have a meeting with the Mayor this evening, but before I left I just wanted to remind you that it's his pre-election party tomorrow night.'

Of course. She'd been so focussed on counting down to the election itself—and the end of their fortnight,

which loomed in her mind like an approaching storm—
that she'd forgotten. 'The one you wish me to attend?'

The one that Stephanos would have a blue fit if she
didn't attend, Rion thought. People had been asking for
her at every event since the meeting. And if she could
have been trusted there was no doubt that her presence
would have had a positive impact. But the fact that the
words *blackmail* or *divorce* could have dropped from her
lips at any time had been too much of a risk. Besides
which, just the knowledge that she was waiting at home
had been distraction enough, never mind having her by
his side all day long. But tomorrow night he had no
choice. *Not* having her there was out of the question. He
was just going to have to keep an eye on her. And himself.

'That's the one. We're also required to stay at the
mayoral residence whilst the election takes place the following day. You will join me?'

For the first time ever her submissive answer came
naturally. A whole evening in which to play meek and
mindless, followed by the night spent together? It would
be the final test.

'Certainly,' she said in that sickly sweet voice.
'Nothing would please me more.'

CHAPTER NINE

WHAT to wear had caused her something of a dilemma. The cobbled together, little-woman-at-home look she'd been sporting for the last week had successfully failed to attract his interest. But tonight he wanted her to be the little woman on his arm, and that demanded an evening dress.

She'd only brought one. In fact, since evenings on Kate's Escapes tours were invariably smart-casual—save for the rare occasions when she covered the Austrian trip, which took in the opera in Vienna—it was also the only one she owned. It was made of a soft, floaty fabric in an ethereal sort of blue. It was perfectly appropriate for the occasion, but it fitted every inch of her body so closely, had always felt so distinctively 'her', that wearing it when she was supposed to be aiming for clichéd felt distinctly inappropriate.

But it was how you acted, not how you looked, which aroused him that afternoon, she reassured herself as she walked down the stairs, eyes deferentially downcast. But not so downcast that she failed to notice the incredible sight of him in his tux, which sent a powerful ripple of longing beneath her skin.

'So is the Mayor at this pre-election party the same Mayor you wanted me to meet at the theatre that night?' she asked, swallowing hard as he led the way to the Bugatti.

Her words interrupted Rion's thoughts—thoughts which involved rucking up her sexy little dress and arriving very late to meet the Mayor indeed. He forced them from his mind. Tonight, of all nights, he needed to stay focussed.

He nodded as he held open the car door for her. 'His name is Georgios Tsamis. Here in Metameikos the role of Mayor is an honorary one rather than one that carries any political power—deservedly bestowed upon Georgios for fighting for his country in the past, and his subsequent work in the local community.'

Libby threw all her efforts into listening, and *not* looking at his powerful hands on the steering wheel as he turned the key in the ignition.

'It has always been the tradition that prior to a new election the Mayor holds a party at his residence, for both the candidates and the voters, as a celebration of democracy and to show that he supports whoever the people elect.'

She nodded her head thoughtfully as they began to zip through the streets towards the new part of Metameikos, daylight just clinging around the edges of the whitewashed villas as the sun began to set. 'But presumably there is always speculation as to which candidate he favours?'

Rion was surprised by her political astuteness. 'Indeed.'

'And he has supported Spyros in previous years?'

'Georgios is a good man, with very traditional values. Unfortunately he is also an extremely poor judge of character and has been oblivious to Spyros's underhand dealings for years.'

Libby wanted to retort that maybe he shouldn't be so quick to complain about a mayor unable to see through people's guises, but she kept her lips tightly locked together and simply nodded.

Rion added nothing further, and a tension similar to the one she'd felt the last time they were in the car together seemed to return as the silence stretched out. Which had to be the product of her imagination, Libby decided, because that had been sexual tension, and even if he *did* keep shooting her sideways glances that looked far from chaste, it couldn't be that, because she hadn't been insubordinate in the least.

Out of the corner of his eye Rion caught her gnawing at her bottom lip with the same frustration that had been eating away at him for days. She wasn't going to hold out much longer. He could feel it. Could feel her trying to convince herself that the atmosphere between them was in her imagination, and the slow dawning realisation that it was not.

He smiled as he rolled the car to a halt outside the mayoral residence and gently ran the back of his hand down her bare arm.

'We're here,' he breathed, feeling her melt beneath his touch.

Instantly, a valet came to open the doors of the Bugatti, and Rion went round to her side of the car ready to escort her in.

She couldn't fail to notice the irony as Rion handed his keys and a hefty tip to the young man in the red-and-grey uniform. Couldn't fail to be reminded of back then, when *he* had been the valet. She dropped her head, the memory of a simpler time, when she'd been convinced that he cared for her, tearing at her heart.

Rion instantly saw the change in her body language. She'd been on the verge of sinking into him, raising her lips to his and giving in. Then she'd caught sight of the valet and her whole demeanour had changed.

Anger coursed through his veins. Red-hot. Relentless. And too instinctive to realise that it was also ill-advised.

He grabbed her wrist and spun her round to face him.

'It doesn't matter how often you remind yourself of what I am, or how hard you try to convince yourself that I'm the one whose desire is an inconvenient truth, it's *never* going to go away.'

Libby's head shot up and her heart began to pound in her ears. 'What are you talking about?'

'This.'

His arm came around her back to hold her steady, encouraging her to arch slightly, so that the whole column of her throat was exposed and her head lay back at the perfect angle for him to take her mouth.

It was hard, punishing, and sexy as hell.

And Libby didn't have a clue what it meant. She

tried to unravel what he'd said, but her mind was too fuzzy with desire—the desire she'd kept locked up for days, but which was now spilling out and into their kiss. It made no sense. He wasn't supposed to desire her when she was being compliant—unless he was so frustrated that she was repressing the woman she'd been that afternoon and he wanted to let her out.

But then he broke away from her, and when the world stopped spinning she realised in horror where they were. Surrounded by the people of Metameikos, all heading towards the soaring mayoral residence before them, all witnessing their public display of affection. She blushed furiously, but it wasn't the dent to her modesty which hurt. It was the realisation that *they* were the reason he'd kissed her. It stung so badly that she forgot she was supposed to be being demure.

'Oh, of course,' she said acidly. 'We're in public again.'

Rion's mouth hardened. 'And what? You think you can use that as an excuse to keep pretending that what's between us isn't real?

'No. I think I've spent the last week being exactly the kind of wife you thought you wanted me to be, but it hasn't appealed to you in the slightest.'

He looked her in the eye, knowing his comeback could be a dire mistake, but too incensed to let it go. 'Or maybe that's just what I let you think.'

Libby stared at him, fresh horror crashing through her, demolishing everything.

He'd *known* what she was trying to do, and he'd spotted that so long as he left her to it he would get exactly what he wanted—a wife 'gracing the marital home' for the duration of his campaign. She felt sick. How had she spent the last week failing to see that he was using her *again*? That light at the end of the tunnel—that glimpse of the Rion she remembered—had been a mirage after all. He *did* just want to control her.

'Ah! Mr Delikaris.' Libby spun round to see an old man who looked a bit like Father Christmas in black tie approaching them. 'And this beautiful young woman must be your wife.' He smiled at her benevolently.

Rion nodded. 'This is Libby. Libby, it's my great pleasure to introduce Georgios Tsamis.'

For the first time in her life Libby was grateful that social niceties had been so drummed into her as a child that they came naturally, even now, when her mind was in complete disarray. She held out her hand. 'It's a pleasure to meet you.'

'And mine to meet you,' Georgios said sincerely. 'And may I say—if you don't mind—how pleased I am to hear that the two of you have recently been reunited.' He leaned towards them with a wink. 'What a joy it is to see two people so in love.'

Libby's nausea rose with a vengeance. Oh, of course—Rion wouldn't have put himself through kissing her just for the benefit of a few citizens. He must have seen the Mayor approaching from a distance and timed his move exactly.

'The staff here will see that your bags are taken to your room,' Georgios explained, looking over to where the valets were carefully parking cars and loading luggage onto trolleys. 'And if you make your way through the main atrium you will see that food and drinks are being served in the Rose Garden. Anything else you need, please just ask. For the next twenty-four hours I want you to think of this as your home.'

'Thank you.' Rion smiled, pressing his hand stiffly into the small of Libby's back. 'I'm sure we will.'

'Wonderful.' Georgios beamed. 'Now, if you'll excuse me…' He looked a little sheepish. 'Mr and Mrs Spyros have just arrived.'

Rion's face was the picture of civility. 'Of course.' He nodded, motioning for him to go ahead and take his leave.

'How convenient that Georgios is such a poor judge of character,' Libby hissed as they walked through the main house towards the garden. 'Else it would have been obvious that I'm only here because you're blackmailing me.'

Rion's whole body tensed. He glanced around to check whether anyone else was in earshot, but thankfully no one seemed to have heard. Yet. *Gamoto!* Thanks to his damned pride, he'd tripled the risk of having her here—and for what?

He swooped on two glasses of rosé from the tray of a passing waitress, handed one to Libby, and took a large gulp of his own. But just as he was about to attempt some serious damage control, Eurycleia came bounding towards them.

'Oh, how delightful to see you both!' She kissed them both affectionately on each cheek. 'Now, I know you've probably got a hundred important people to see this evening, but I just *had* to come over and see that you're well.' She furrowed her brow in motherly concern. 'Is there anything you need? I can bring round some more biscuits if you're short. I'd only need to pop in for a minute—'

'Thank you for the kind offer,' Rion interrupted, 'but Libby's been keeping us fully stocked in the biscuit department.'

Eurycleia clapped her hands together in delight. 'Oh, but of course—just as it should be.' She turned back to Rion. 'Though you mustn't let her spend too much time in the kitchen. A woman must have her own life too, you know.'

'My thoughts exactly,' Libby replied gravely. 'And I have no doubt that Rion will soon have every reason to beg for your return.'

Rion scowled at her as Eurycleia's face lit up.

'You just enjoy your time off,' he said gruffly, then tilted his head to look at the man watching her from across the lawn with a twinkle in his eye. 'I don't doubt Petros is keeping you busy.'

Eurycleia looked back at him and rolled her eyes affectionately. 'I dare say he is.'

'He looks as though he really dotes on you,' Libby added. She'd meant it to come out jovially, but she could hear the wistfulness in her own voice. Thankfully, neither Eurycleia nor Rion seemed to notice.

'Oh, he's just come over all protective because I've been talking to that charming young man who works for you,' Eurycleia said to Rion. 'Now, what's his name…?

Stephanos? Yes, that's it. He was telling me how you and he-who-I-shan't-even-name are now neck and neck in the opinion polls. I mean, really, as if a young man like that is going to be interested in me!'

She threw her hands in the air in exasperation, and then clapped them back together again.

'Oh, listen to me—waffling on. I've already taken up too much of your precious time.' She reached out to squeeze their hands in turn. 'If you need anything, you know where to find me.' She winked, held up two sets of crossed fingers, and then scuttled back across the lawn.

Libby watched her go, taking in the garden's swirling mix of fairylights and flowers for the first time. It reminded her of some of the parties her parents had held in the grounds of Ashworth Manor—the ones where they'd invited every wealthy family in the south of England with sons about her age. But here there was no such discrimination; the designer-clad of the new town were mixed with the home-made Sunday best of the old town, exactly the way she would have preferred those other parties to have been. Yes, she recognised that some people didn't look a hundred per cent comfortable in their surroundings, but save for a few of Spyros's clan everyone seemed to be making the effort to mingle.

In fact, it looked exactly what it was supposed to be: a celebration of democracy. Except it wasn't, was it? she thought miserably. Democracy was about the freedom to choose, but the people of Metameikos had no choice. This election was between one deceptive, power-hungry fat cat and another; she had no doubt about that now. And she couldn't bear the thought of being a part of it.

She took a swig of wine from the glass in her hand and turned back to face him. 'I told you from the start, Rion, I'm not prepared to lie for you. Especially when as far as I can see you're no better than Spyros.'

Rion gritted his teeth. 'I'm not asking you to lie for me.'

'You're asking me to stand by your side and look like I want to be there. That's a lie.'

'Is it?' he murmured scathingly. 'It didn't feel like you ever wanted to be anywhere else when you were making love to me.'

Libby shook her head wretchedly. 'And that became a lie the second you used it as nothing more than an aid to your campaign.'

Rion's anger turned to puzzlement, and then his face stilled. 'When I rang the office I told them I'd missed the call because the meeting overran, that was all.'

Her cheeks flushed. God, she wanted to believe him. But how could she? He'd say whatever it took to stop her from leaving, from ruining his chances of success. He had done so from the start.

'No.' She shook her head again, more fiercely, and felt her whole body begin to sway from side to side. She took a step backwards, but he grabbed onto her wrist and pressed his lips to her ear.

'You want honesty, Libby? The truth is this isn't about the election, or what it says about our marriage on paper. This is about you and me. It always has been—'

'No!' She wrenched herself away from him so

fiercely that a sharp pain shot through her shoulder. She'd believed that for so long, but tonight just proved that was the biggest lie of all. 'I can't do this, Rion!'

She had to go. If she didn't, her poor battered heart might never recover.

She was surprised he didn't haul her back and physically bar her escape, but as she began to dart through the crowds, clattering her half-empty wine glass onto a passing silver tray, she supposed it made sense. Holding his wife by force would do even more damage to his precious reputation than her absence altogether.

She didn't know where she was going, except to somewhere wide and free and as far from him as possible—which meant away from here. But, just as she was about to run into the main house and back through the door they'd used to come in, she spotted a side passage by a laurel tree, to the far left of the building, which had initially been obscured as she'd crossed the garden. From this angle, it looked as if it would lead back to the road a lot more quickly, and cut out the possibility of her running into anyone she knew.

She quickly made her way towards it, but just as she was about to turn into the passageway she heard hushed voices and stopped dead in her tracks.

'Come on—I hardly think pocket money is going to cut it. I'll have to close their precious museum and turf at least fifty of them out of their homes.'

It took her a few moments to place it, but as she concealed herself alongside the tree she realised that the sly, unpleasant voice belonged to Spyros.

Ever so slowly, clutching on to the trunk so that she could lean forward without making a sound, Libby peered down the passageway. She could just make out a lanky man she didn't recognise removing a roll of notes from the inside of his jacket pocket and adding it to the bulge already in his hand.

'That's more like it,' Spyros declared lustily.

The man continued to cling onto the cash, despite Spyros's outstretched palm. 'And the planning permission?' he said expectantly.

'Will be on your desk by the end of the week.'

The man looked annoyed. 'And what if you are no longer in charge of Metameikos by the end of this week?'

Libby saw Spyros flinch and run his chubby forefinger around the back of his collar.

'You think I'm worried about Delikaris?' He forced a laid-back laugh. 'A boy from the slums who thinks a new hospital will bring back his brother?'

Libby's eyes widened in disbelief. Brother? What brother?

'But even Stamos said he was beginning to think that—'

'Do you want to build your luxury apartments or not?

Libby strained to hear, strained not to cough.

And then suddenly a hand grasped her waist from behind.

CHAPTER TEN

LIBBY gave a yelp as she was lifted off the ground, limbs thrashing helplessly. But as her assailant dragged her past the laurel tree and through a gate in the wall an unmistakable scent filled her nostrils. Rion's.

'Put me down!' She struggled out of his grip, her relief swiftly turning to anger. 'I just saw something!'

She tried to dart back through the gate of the smaller walled garden they now found themselves in, but Rion placed his hands on her upper arms, easily restraining her. 'I guessed.'

'Spyros,' she said breathlessly, 'taking a bribe…to pass planning permission for some luxury apartments…in the old town.'

His face remained unmoved. 'Like I said, he's corruption personified.'

'If we go back now I can tell everyone what I've seen!'

Rion said nothing, simply continued to hold her there. She found it so maddening that she tried to push past him a second time. But when he held her firm again she forced herself to question why, and suddenly it was obvious.

Running back into the main garden screaming treason at the eleventh hour would do more harm to Rion's reputation than to Spyros's. The fastest, most effective way of putting an end to his corruption wasn't to slander him, it was to beat him in the polls.

Libby's eyes remained on Rion's face, dimly illuminated in the pale moonlight. Ten minutes ago she hadn't been able to bear the thought of staying here a second longer, had believed it would make no difference who won. But now she had unequivocal proof that Spyros was everything Rion said he was. And Rion?

She took a deep breath, hating that she had to ask such a basic question of the man she'd been married to for five years. 'Spyros said something else too…something about you having a brother.'

'What about my brother?' he shot out, his voice loaded with venom.

So it was true. Part of her heart soared at the possibility that he was driven by something other than just power and success. The other part wished it *had* been a lie, because it proved that even now there was still so much they didn't know about one another. But most of all she wished it wasn't true because she could see the pain in his eyes and it tore at her heart.

She chose her words carefully. 'He said you wanted to build the new hospital because of him.'

Rion said nothing, simply continued to stare out into the darkness.

'It's true, then?' she ventured after several moments.

He gritted his teeth. Thanks to that creep Spyros it

looked as if he had no choice but to tell her, did he? Not that it mattered. It wasn't as if he could fall any lower in her estimation. Besides, she'd already made up her mind that she was leaving.

He nodded sharply. 'His name was Jason. We were twins.'

Twins? They'd been even more than brothers, then. Libby looked up into his face. It felt as if she was seeing him for the first time. 'What happened?'

'He caught pneumonia the winter we both turned twelve.' He mistook her frown of sorrow for one of incomprehension. 'Mum, Jason and I—my father left before we were even born—shared a place with another family. Eurycleia's,' he explained abruptly. 'It was damp, freezing cold, and a wonder any of us survived.'

Libby's eyes fluttered down to meet her cheeks. *Whilst you grew up in the log-fire warmth of Ashworth Manor,* she added to herself, knowing that was what he was thinking and suddenly racked with guilt for ever bemoaning her upbringing. Was that why he'd always coveted the house where he lived now? Not because it was the most luxurious in Metameikos but because it was the perfect family home?

'We took him to hospital, where we were told to wait,' Rion continued, his voice loaded with bitterness. 'And we waited. Whilst every other patient, no matter how trivial their condition, nor what time they'd arrived, was seen before us. On the third day Jason was the only one left in the waiting room. But the doctors still refused to see him.'

Libby winced as the grossly inappropriate sound of laughter from the party drifted over the wall.

'They wanted their palms greased. Believed, I suppose, that my mother would find the money.' He shook his head. 'She worked day and night for a pittance, just to be able to feed and clothe us. She had nothing to give but a few coins and a mother's love, and no friends or relatives with anything more.' A look of pain began to cloud Rion's eyes. 'In her desperation she did the only thing she could think of. She went to Spyros's father— the leader of Metameikos at the time—to beg for help.' The look of torment was instantly replaced by one of loathing. 'He told her that life, like everything else, had a price. He was right. Jason died right there in the waiting room.'

Libby's heart twisted in empathy. She wanted to go to him and wrap her arms around him, but he was looking at her as if there was no way she could ever understand. And in a way maybe she couldn't.

'My mother almost died of grief,' he went on. 'I believe that was what killed her in the end, but it would have happened ten years earlier if we'd stayed here. Eurycleia's husband worked on the docks; he helped us stow away to England.'

'I'm sorry,' Libby whispered, but the words had never seemed more inadequate. She was sorry for so much: that he'd been through all that; that her assumptions about why he was doing this had been so far off the mark; that she hadn't given him her support when his motives were so admirable.

Rion looked at her resentfully. 'I don't want your pity, Libby.'

No, she could tell he didn't want her to know, full-stop. Yet wasn't it obvious that if he had explained the real reason he wanted to win this election from the start she would have automatically wanted to help him succeed?

Yes, she thought, it probably was, but he clearly found the prospect of her staying because she felt sorry for him abhorrent. Just like the prospect of winning this election for the same reason, she realised suddenly. Spyros knew about Jason because of his father, but no one else did, did they? If they did, Rion would have no need to convince them of his commitment to family values, to Metameikos—but he'd chosen to avoid the sympathy vote.

'You don't have my pity,' she whispered, needing him to believe that her support had nothing to do with that and everything to do with believing in justice, believing in him. The corners of her mouth turned downwards. 'Are you telling me this kind of thing is still happening here now?'

He spoke through gritted teeth. 'Spyros Junior has had to get more subtle about it, but the divide between rich and poor is as wide as it ever was.'

'I had no idea.' How naïve her idealistic view of the old town had been, how small-minded to think that indifference was responsible for his reticence. She shook her head, ashamed. 'I thought that you just wanted the power…the success.'

'And now you know it's about the street urchin wanting his revenge?'

Libby stared at him. But it wasn't that, was it? He could have exacted his vengeance on the doctors or on the Spyros family in any number of ways, but he'd decided to take the high road, to make things better for the next generation.

Suddenly they were interrupted by the sound of something metal being chinked against something glass on the other side of the wall, then a hushed silence, which was followed by a loud voice.

'Ladies and gentlemen, Mayor Tsamis will be giving the traditional toast to the candidates in the main hall in five minutes.'

Immediately the shutters came up on Rion's face. 'I need to go.'

Of course he did. As Libby watched him turn on his heel, without even glancing back to see whether she had any intention of joining him, she knew she needed to go too. Not away from here, but inside, with him. Because the freedom he stood for was the very thing she'd spent *her* whole life fighting for.

And because she finally had the proof that he *was* the inherently good man she'd fallen in love with after all.

Rion stood at the front of the main hall beside Stephanos and stared bleakly into the glass of champagne he'd just been handed.

Libby was gone, long gone, he had no doubt about that. She'd known he was poor, that he had no connections, but the horror in her eyes when he'd told her the sordid details of his past had been palpable. If her plan earlier had been to walk away, she'd probably sprinted halfway back to Athens by now.

Anger burned in his throat. Anger at her—for leaving him. Twice. Anger at himself for believing deep down he might be able to seduce her into staying, for even wanting to try. Most of all for jeopardising everything by supposing this could ever have worked.

Stephanos stood beside him, anxiously leaning back to look for her through the crowd as Georgios ascended the podium. Out of the corner of his eye Rion could see Spyros's fat stomach protruding from either side of his scarlet cummerbund as he did the same, only the expression he wore was one of glee.

Georgios tapped a fork against his wine glass and the room fell silent.

'Good evening, ladies and gentleman, and thank you all for coming. It's a great pleasure to see so many of you here on the eve of what is set to be the closest and without a doubt the most exciting election we have seen in Metameikos for many years.'

'Hear, hear,' Rion heard a female voice which sounded a lot like Eurycleia's call out from the crowd. Spyros's face turned to thunder.

'Over the course of their campaigns both candidates and their teams have worked tirelessly in new and innovative ways to listen to your views and broadcast their policies, and I'm delighted to be able to say that when I stand before you tomorrow with the results I am sure that, no matter what the outcome, you will be guaranteed a leader who will give his all to Metameikos.'

But all of what? That was the question, Rion thought grimly.

'Which leaves me, without further ado, to raise a toast to the candidates, and to their wive—'

Georgios looked down to pick them out in the crowd, and spotted immediately that Libby was missing. Rion's heart stopped beating in his chest. Excuses hovered on his tongue—she'd been taken suddenly ill, there'd been a family emergency—but he couldn't bring himself to utter any of them. Because he couldn't stop recalling the accusation of dishonesty that Libby had levelled at him earlier. Wanting her by his side *hadn't* been a lie, but saying any one of those excuses aloud, however well-intentioned, would be. And if he won the election based on deceit, *wouldn't* that make him just as reprehensible as Spyros?

But just as Rion was about to open his mouth and declare the truth he noticed that the heads of the crowd were all turning towards the door. And then they parted.

Libby.

She looked so nymph-like as she floated in in her pale blue dress that for a moment Rion was convinced that what he was seeing was actually an apparition.

But then she spoke. 'My apologies, Mr Tsamis. For a moment the events of this evening were a little overwhelming.'

'Completely understandable, my dear.' Georgios smiled as she went to stand beside her husband. 'No need to apologise.'

Georgios turned his focus back to the crowd. 'And

now that we are all present and correct, it gives me great pleasure to raise a—'

'You were busy forming an opinion on your husband's policies, perhaps?' Spyros suddenly interrupted, turning viciously on Libby. 'For I hear that the last time you were asked you declared you needed more time to make up your mind. I'm sure I'm not the only one here who thinks you should be given a fresh opportunity to express your views.'

Libby was so startled by his breach of etiquette that it took a few seconds for his hypocrisy to hit home. But no longer than that. She took a deep breath, suppressed the urge to share with the crowd what she'd witnessed in the passageway earlier, and turned on her well-pefected, sickly-sweet voice instead.

'Why, thank you, Spyros. Whilst I'm not sure that now is the time—' she lowered her head respectfully towards Georgios '—I'm pleased you feel so strongly about people's views being heard.' She caught the eye of Eurycleia a few rows back. She clearly hadn't missed the note of sarcasm in her voice and was grinning jubilantly.

'You are correct that when I arrived just under two weeks ago I'd had little time to consider my feelings on any policies. What was more, I believed that no one could know what Metameikos needed better than its people themselves. I still believe that. But now I'm certain of one thing. Orion Delikaris is not the man you think he is.' She paused, and heard him suck in a breath beside her. 'Orion is *one* of the people. He hasn't just flown in from Athens with a bunch of policies he's plucked out of thin air because he thinks they're the ones that will gain him the most votes; this is his home. His policies are born out of the same desire for a better, fairer Metameikos that everyone here—' She stopped and looked directly at Spyros. 'That *almost* everyone here shares. They're more than just policies; they're the promises he's already made to himself.'

There weren't the whoops and cheers she'd got at the meeting this time. Instead there was a kind of silent awe, a collective hope.

Georgios smiled at her and gently bowed his head. 'Thank you, Mrs Delikaris. Now, lest we should all be quizzed—' he glared at Spyros, whose expression was one of complete and utter horror '—I should like to finally raise that toast: to the candidates of this year's election, and their wives.'

'The candidates and their wives,' the crowd repeated, raising their glasses.

'And may the best man win.'

As Georgios descended from the podium amidst a round of applause, Rion stared at Libby, dumbfounded. Yes, he knew precisely what she'd meant when she'd described him as *one of the people*, but she'd nevertheless done everything in her power to help him.

It was the last thing he'd expected, but now he thought about it—about her reaction when she'd overheard Spyros, the things she'd said before about witnessing injustice around the world—he supposed it did add up. *She* might not want to be married to a man of his background, but it seemed she had compassion for those who could hope for nothing more.

'Thank you,' he whispered stiltedly in her ear as the crowd began to disperse.

Libby inclined her head in gratitude as they headed back towards the garden, but she didn't allow herself to *feel* glad until Stephanos and the other members of his team came over to rejoice in the good fortune of Spyros's outburst and the quick-wittedness of her response. Not because she wanted their thanks—Rion's meant far more—but because she knew that unless she kept her guard up when she was alone with him she was in serious danger of telling him that she was in love with him.

Which, she told herself as the party continued in a blur of introductions, small talk and sipped champagne, would be an exceptionally foolish thing to do. Because she might have proof that all along he had been motivated by good, but she had no evidence that he'd retained any of the feelings that had once prompted him to propose all those years ago, or that he was capable of understanding why she'd left and moved forward. On the contrary, if their original agreement still stood—and he'd given her no indication that it didn't—then tomorrow he would sign the divorce papers and be done with her.

By the time the crowds began to thin, and Libby found herself alone with him again, she'd almost built her defences back up.

'Come on,' he whispered, inclining his head towards the house. 'We've done everything we can.'

Libby was glad. Her feet were sore and the muscles in her cheeks had begun to ache. Whilst she'd genuinely enjoyed talking to many of the local people, the awareness that she was being scrutinised had induced a kind of facial fatigue she hadn't experienced since those parties at Ashworth Manor.

Yet her relief was accompanied by trepidation. Georgios was bound to have reserved them a double room, and unless she wanted to undo all their hard work tonight she had no choice but to stay in it—with Rion. And, whilst she'd spent the evening schooling her heart against him, she knew that would do her about as much good as a map of Metameikos in Malaga if he came anywhere near her.

'Ah, Mr and Mrs Delikaris.' She heard Georgios's voice behind them as they walked through the atrium. 'You're off to bed? Not a moment too soon. Tomorrow is going to be a long day for you both.' He lowered his voice and came in between them, placing his arms around their shoulders. 'Come. I would prefer it if you kept this to yourselves, but I have reserved you the best room in the house.'

So good it had two beds? Libby wondered optimistically.

Georgios pressed a key into Rion's hand and guided them down the main corridor that led off of the hallway, and then along a narrower one to the right, where the high walls were covered from floor to ceiling in beautiful neoclassical paintings.

Libby spun around, her concerns temporarily forgotten as she looked up in awe. 'Is this part of the residence open to the public?' she asked, wondering if she'd reached her conclusion that the new part of the town had nothing worth visiting too quickly.

'Yes, of course,' Georgios answered. 'The mayoral residence really *belongs* to the people of Metameikos. The Mayor has permission to add to it—this wing was built by a mayor named Leander back in the eighteenth century, whilst the one we are headed to now was constructed by my predecessor—but really we're just its guardians.'

She nodded in appreciation. 'I'm a tour guide,' she explained. 'I run excursions for small groups. I'd love to add a trip here to the itinerary I'm currently working on.'

Georgios looked delighted, but at the same time perplexed. 'And you enjoy your work?'

'Yes,' Libby said sincerely. 'I love it.'

He turned to Rion, rolled his eyes and threw his hands in the air. 'Just like my wife! All my life I do the honourable thing—work hard so that she doesn't have to—and then she insists on getting a job! I never understood it.'

His words forced Libby to do a double-take. What had he just said?

That he'd always tried to do the honourable thing and support his wife, and that he'd never been able to understand her desire to work?

Rapidly, Georgios's words seeped into her mind, changing the colour of the past. After she and Rion had married she'd thought that he wanted to make his own way in the world, buy a better house, without any contribution from her. When he'd refused to admit that, she'd been convinced he was in denial, but suddenly she thought she understood. It hadn't been a question of ambition, it had been a question of honour. And what had she done? Walked away.

As a whole new wave of guilt washed over her, Libby failed to notice that they'd slowed right down and that Georgios had just hit a square gold button in the wall. Because it had just occurred to her where that code of honour came from. It wasn't just that he was Greek, it was that he'd had to watch helplessly as his mother had had to work day and night to support him and his brother.

And suddenly she saw why he had never comprehended that working and living alone was what she needed to feel free. Because freedom to his mother would have been a home, a husband to support her. Her heart turned over. Everything he'd given *her.*

Suddenly a loud *ping* broke through her thoughts. 'Here we are. It's on the top floor, straight in front of you as you exit the lift.'

Lift? Libby felt her pulse-rate rocket.

'Um, I'd really rather take the stairs, if you don't mind,' she shot out abruptly, desperately flicking her eyes past Georgios and around the new wing, looking for a stairwell. 'Walk off all those delicious hors d'oeuvres.'

Rion eyed her quizzically, unable to fathom her expression. She was probably just worried about what she might do if she found herself in an enclosed space with him. Good.

Georgios shook his head and tutted. 'My son married an English girl too—barely eats a lettuce leaf! Hasn't Rion told you that Greek men don't like their women too skinny? Particularly if it means a longer journey to the bedroom.' He chuckled softly, ushering her forward as the doors opened and Rion thanked him for his hospitality.

She wanted to back away from the lift, to have Rion look at her, automatically understand, and endorse her suggestion that they take the stairs—but then he still didn't know some fundamental things about her, did he? And what would it say about their marriage to Georgios if she suddenly blurted out something like that now?

'Sleep well,' Georgios called after them as the doors slowly closed.

The second they shut Libby's heart began to thunder in her chest and her breaths became short, sharp and raspy.

'Are you okay?'

'I don't do lifts,' she choked, pushing her hand up against the doors, leaning her head into the crook of her elbow and focussing on the crack, willing it to open.

Instantly Rion saw her words were an understatement and put his hands on her shoulders. He spun her round. 'You're claustrophobic?'

She nodded.

Gamoto! He hit every button on the lift's panel to try and make it stop—at any floor he could. Why hadn't she told him downstairs? He bent his knees slightly, so that his eyes were level with hers. Because if she had Georgios would have known something was amiss, he realised suddenly. A wave of guilt coursed through him.

They both quickly realised it was one of those lifts which obeyed commands in order and was going all the way up to the top floor first.

Visions of the walls closing in around her began to flood Libby's mind, her temperature soared, and then the muscles in her neck went so weak that her chin lolled against her chest.

'No,' he said, firmly but gently. 'I need you to keep looking at me.'

He placed his hands on either side of her face and guided her head upwards, so that her eyes were level with his again.

'We're not here,' he said, very definitely, searching her face for inspiration, needing a memory he could use to transport her mind away from there. Somewhere open, out-of-doors, where they'd both been together. He was momentarily struck by how tragic it was that there was such a lack of options, even from the months of their marriage they'd spent together, but he didn't have time to dwell on what that meant.

'We're in Athens,' he said suddenly. 'We're in Athens and it's snowing.' *All right, the options are limited, Delikaris, but surely you could have thought of something other than that?*

The tension in Libby's chest, the growing movement towards the black hole was immediately immobilised. Had he just said Athens? In the snow?

Rion couldn't miss the way her whole body seemed to pull back from the brink just a fraction. Oh, what the hell? If it took her mind off this... Reminding her that even their wedding day had been a let-down was hardly going to make any difference after all that he'd been forced to reveal tonight.

'We're slowly making our way to the town hall—on foot, through the National Gardens, because the taxi can't make it up the road.'

'They haven't got round to clearing it yet,' she whispered, her words slurring into each other a little at first. 'But a few people are just starting to come outside with shovels.' The memories seemed to form a dam in her mind, holding back the rising panic.

'And we manage to talk an old man and woman into coming with us to witness the ceremony—'

'In exchange for the promise of hot chocolate.'

To Rion's astonishment she smiled—and it wasn't tinged with any of the distaste he would have expected. Only because she'd temporarily lost control of her faculties, he was sure, but for a second he allowed himself to forget that.

'They thought we were crazy.' He smiled too.

We were hung in the air. But neither of them said it.

Suddenly the lift made that pinging sound again and the doors opened.

But Libby barely even registered it, because she was looking at him with tears in her eyes and she couldn't look away.

CHAPTER ELEVEN

'WE'RE here.'

His words broke the spell. Libby blinked hard, forced the tears back behind her eyes, and looked down at her feet. To her astonishment she realised they were still firmly planted inside the lift. Even though the doors were wide open. *How was that even possible?*

'Are you okay to walk?'

She nodded, not entirely sure that she was.

Rion looped his arm through hers and encouraged her out onto the landing, but she couldn't focus forward. She kept looking back over her shoulder, trying to work out what the hell had just happened. How could she have felt less restricted in a small space with another person than she would have done alone?

'You're okay,' he whispered, mistaking her backward glance for a look of trepidation. 'I promise we'll take the stairs from now on.'

Oh, she was scared, all right, but she didn't think the kind of fear she was feeling now could be eradicated by avoiding enclosed spaces.

He delved into his jacket pocket for the key as they reached a large wooden door. 'At least our room is bound to be spacious.'

Her vision was still a little blurry, but when he unlocked the door there was no mistaking that it was. Nor was there any mistaking that, despite its gargantuan dimensions, there was only the one bed. An enormous four-poster bed, bedecked with crisp cream sheets and decadent aubergine drapes. It stood in the middle of the room, staring back at them like an enormous question mark. Or at least that was how it seemed to Libby.

'You should sit down,' he said, his voice raspy. She had a feeling the bed seemed that way to him too.

He strode across to the windows, which stretched the length of the opposite wall, and opened a couple to let in the cool evening breeze. Then he disappeared through a doorway at the far end of the room.

Libby was still standing dazedly in the same spot when he returned, carrying a glass of water.

'Here.' He swapped the glass for the handbag she was still clutching in her right hand, and dipped his head in the direction of the bed, his voice more insistent this time. 'Sit.'

Libby did as he commanded whilst he pulled up a chair, shrugged off his jacket and sat down facing her.

'When did it start?'

She tried to sound breezy, raising the glass to her lips to take a sip of water. 'Oh, you know—when do all these things start? When I was a kid.'

'When you were *a child*?' She felt him strain not to

raise his voice. 'How did I not know about this?' He shook his head as if her answer wouldn't compute. 'We lived on the fourth floor!'

'We didn't exactly enter or leave the apartment together very frequently,' she said quietly. 'Besides, the lift was usually out of order.'

Rion smarted, but let it go. 'Do you know what started it in the first place?'

Libby drew in a short, sharp breath, not wanting to make a big deal out of it. Especially now that she knew it was nothing compared to what he'd gone through in *his* childhood. 'I think being locked in the cupboard below the stairs for hours at a time if I displeased my father had something to do with it.'

Rion balled his hand into a fist and fought the urge to take out his anger on an inanimate object in the absence of Thomas Ashworth himself. *Gamoto!* Ever since he'd learned that her father had kept her cut off, even after their separation, he'd known he was more than just a bigot. But this was something else. 'You should have told me.'

She exhaled deeply. 'I did try—in my own way.'

But maybe she should have tried harder, Libby thought for the first time as she registered the look of shock on his face. Because she'd never sat him down and made him understand what was at the root of her need to feel free and in control, any more than he'd told *her* about where his drive to provide for them really came from. They'd just both thought the other should understand instinctively, and she'd bolted when they hadn't.

She shook her head, the tragedy of it piercing her heart as she realised how different things might have been if they'd known. But then again, maybe not. Because how could they have fought each other's demons when they hadn't been done fighting their own?

'*When* did you try and tell me?' he demanded.

He knew there was no way he'd forget a detail like that. She'd never once mentioned any fear of— Libby looked up at him with wide eyes, and suddenly the bottom dropped out of his stomach. Her expression took him right back to the day she'd walked away. No, she hadn't mentioned a fear of enclosed spaces specifically, but she had always been desperate not to be left alone in that apartment, to go out and get a job and—

Rion squeezed his eyes tightly shut. But that had been because she couldn't bear living in that hovel, hadn't it? Suddenly the memory mixed with what Georgios had said downstairs, about his wife *wanting* to get a job. Libby *had* only ever spoken of working with pleasure. And, come to think of it, she'd never complained about the apartment itself. So had he been wrong? And, if he had been, what the hell else had he got wrong about her?

Nothing, a voice in the back of his mind ground out, refusing to let him go any further down that path and lay himself open to that level of pain all over again. Yes, maybe he *had* been wrong about the reason why she'd wanted to get a job, why she hadn't wanted to be alone in the apartment, but it didn't change the underlying reason why she'd gone. Why she was here now, demanding a divorce. That night after they'd been to the theatre she'd admitted it—she found being his wife *humiliating*. Because in her eyes he'd never, ever be good enough.

He forced his eyes open and stood up. 'I'll get you some more water.'

'No—' She reached out her hand and placed it on his forearm. 'I'm fine, honestly.'

Rion clenched his teeth, just the feel of her fingertips on his skin causing a tightening in his groin. 'Nevertheless, you should get some rest.'

He walked round to the opposite side of the room and Libby heard him turn on the bedside lamp. Her eyes remained fixed on the chair where he'd been sitting. She recognised that last look on his face. It was the one he'd worn that afternoon. He wanted her. He actually wanted her. And it wasn't about control or defiance or the election. She knew it wasn't. It was about those memories. Her heart blossomed. He wanted her, but he was fighting it because he thought she was still unwell, that it wasn't what she wanted.

She drew in a deep breath, his thoughtfulness seeping into her heart, mixing with everything else that she'd discovered about him tonight. And even if she hadn't left all her defences in the lift, then the remainder slid off the bed and slunk out of sight at that moment.

'Rion, I don't want…' She heard him go still behind her, heard the nervous quiver in her own voice. 'I don't want you to fight this. I know I can't. Not tonight.'

The tightness in Rion's groin instantly intensified, but he didn't move, simply carried on staring at the back of her head. Had that moment in the lift weakened her faculties *and* taken her defences with them, then? Or had thinking about her father simply reawakened her desire to rebel by having it off with the boy from nowhere?

It was the admission he'd been waiting for—another chance to wear her down, remind her that they were driven by just the same urges. But tonight he had to wonder whether the only thing he was really wearing down was his self-respect.

'And what about tomorrow, Libby? Your defences will return with the sunrise?'

She turned to face him, her voice barely a whisper. 'No, I doubt I'll be able to fight it then either. Or the next day.'

Triumph flooded through Rion's chest as he realised the depth of her capitulation. She was saying she wouldn't *ever* be able to fight it.

Instantly, what was left of his plot to take revenge went up in smoke. It would never have been satisfying enough anyway. The only thing that could satisfy him was her, returning as his wife, for good. 'Then you'll stay?' he growled. 'After tomorrow?'

Libby stared at him and felt her heart swell to double its normal size.

He was asking her to stay. After the election. When the reason he needed her here would be gone. And the only reason remaining would be because he wanted her to.

Hours ago she'd been sure that leaving was the only sane thing to do. That he would never love her… Now she still had no guarantees, knew they had a mountain to climb, but he had just given her every reason to hope that it *was* possible.

She stood up and walked towards him, emotions washing over her. 'Yes, Rion, I'll stay.'

Rion stared at her in amazement. He'd done it. He'd actually broken her, made her realise that their desire for one another did transcend all else. And he didn't hesitate. Suddenly, definitively, he dropped his head and found her mouth.

Libby revelled in it, roving her hands up his back, hungrily raking her fingers through his hair, then sliding his tie from beneath his collar. She tossed it to the floor while Rion's hands stroked up her arms and then straight back down again, taking the straps of her dress with him and exposing her to the waist.

He let out a growl of pleasure at the discovery that she was not wearing a bra, and stilled for just a moment to watch as her nipples peaked under his gaze. God, she wanted him to look at her like that for ever.

She let out a moan as he lowered his head and began to slick his tongue over her nipples, nuzzling her, caressing her. But the aching need between her thighs made her impatient for more. She ran her hand up his leg, towards the waistband of his trousers, feeling his arousal jump as she skimmed over it, and then encouraged him back towards the bed.

'Wait,' he said, placing his hands on hers and returning them to her. 'Just a second.'

He moved quickly to their bags, which had been neatly placed in the corner of the room, and swiftly unzipped a pocket to extract a condom.

The second Libby realised what he was doing she

knew she had to stop him this time. Yes, it might result in a few moments of awkward explanation, but she understood now that honesty was essential if their marriage was ever going to work. 'No.' She shook her head, gnawing on her lower lip and praying that it wouldn't destroy the moment completely. 'That's not necessary.'

Rion stared down at the foil packet between his fingers, then looked up at her face in astonishment. No, he thought, as the full extent of her capitulation truly sank in. Now she'd agreed to return as his wife permanently, he supposed it *wasn't* necessary, was it?

But the soaring triumph that accompanied the realisation that she'd just suggested the one thing he'd always wanted was curtailed by the look of resignation on her face. Because it was perfectly clear that she didn't deem him any more worthy to be the father of her children now than she had done then. The only difference was that now she understood she was never going to want another man the way she wanted him, and that, unless she was prepared to live without desire like that, his lack of breeding was something she was just going to have to try and forget.

And, whilst his instinct was to pull down the remainder of her dress, spill his seed inside her, and prove that class was irrelevant to Mother Nature, the thought of doing so in such a way that would remind her of his uncivilised roots, of the concession she was having to make, was utterly repugnant to him.

Instead he dropped the condom, inwardly vowed to

keep his philistine urges on a tightly coiled leash, and slowly stalked back to the bed to focus on her pleasure.

'Lie down.'

Libby felt her desire rocket at his husky command and stepped back, slid off the remainder of her dress, and stretched out on the bed in answer. She was surprised that he asked no questions, levelled no accusation of infidelity, but she was glad. She took it as proof that his feelings mirrored hers, that he saw whatever had happened in the intervening years—not that anything *had* happened on her part—as history.

He quickly came to join her on the bed, and Libby felt him run his eyes downwards, over her breasts, across her scrap of underwear and down her legs. But as she looked up into his face to savour his appreciation she was surprised to see that his expression wasn't the one of urgent need she'd expected, instead he looked—detached. *The way he did when your marriage was on its last legs,* a voice taunted in the back of her mind.

But as his mouth homed in on hers once more, she told herself she'd imagined it. He'd just asked her to stay, for goodness' sake, admitted he couldn't fight this any more than she could. Determined to prove it, she rolled over on to her side, splayed her hand across his chest and began butterflying kisses down towards his belly button. But just as she was about to curl her fingers around his length he caught her wrist and shook his head.

She felt an arrow of disappointment fire up inside her chest, but it never got the chance to land. For Rion instantly took his tongue on a sensuous journey of its own, lower and lower, to the point of aching need, until he was tasting her, filling her with such delicious heat that she could do nothing but throw her head back helplessly against the pillows and surrender to a pleasure so agonisingly intense that she wasn't sure whether she wanted to scream for it to stop or for it never to end.

But if she'd supposed she had time to do either, she was mistaken. Because, as she gripped the back of his head in one hand and the sheets with the other, she was already there.

Dizzy with pleasure, but desperate to bring him the same, Libby threw her arm across his middle and encouraged him to move on top of her. Rion's body jolted eagerly, but instead of following her lead he placed his hands around her waist and moved *her* on top of *him*.

Libby didn't complain, convinced his way would be equally effective. She straddled his body and sank down onto him, angling herself forward so that she could move up and down on just the tip of him.

Rion let out an anguished moan and she smiled, taking the whole length of him inside her. He closed his eyes and let his head roll to one side momentarily, but seconds later he snapped his eyes open again, smoothed his hands up her sides, and grazed her nipples with his thumbs. Combined with the feel of their bodies moving together, it created a pleasure so intense that she didn't have the strength to lower her mouth and kiss the sensitive hollow beneath his ear, or to tease him by slowing down the rhythm as she'd planned to, because her body was already tightening again.

And, before she could help herself, suddenly she was drenched in another flood of sensation.

Only when she had finished, and cried out for a second time, did she feel Rion give one final upward thrust and hear a primitive growl tear from his lips. But just as she was revelling in the sound of it he cut it short.

Libby lay down by his side, the arrow of disappointment finally landing in her heart. She tried to stop it, but she couldn't. Because until then she'd been sure that lovemaking was the one area of their marriage which needed no further work. She told herself it still didn't, that he'd just climaxed for heaven's sake, but she knew his passion had been nowhere near as unchecked as it had been that day in the hallway.

She propped herself up on one elbow and looked down into his face, praying for the courage to ask him what the problem was—or, more to the point, the courage to stick around for the answer. But his eyes were closed, and she could hear his breathing growing slower and deeper, verging on the edge of sleep.

And no wonder. Suddenly she felt racked with guilt for being so self-absorbed—especially after an evening in which she'd realised how important it was for them to really try and support and understand one another. Of course he was going to be a little detached tonight. If he wasn't completely exhausted after two tireless weeks of campaigning, then he was probably worrying about the election tomorrow.

After that, everything would be different. She looked over at the bedside clock, realising the polls would be opening in a few hours. Yes, she thought, as the reality of what she had agreed to began to sink in, after that everything would be very different indeed.

CHAPTER TWELVE

LIBBY had never seen a man look so calm and collected. Or a man so impossibly handsome, either, but that went without saying. Everyone else in the main hall seemed unable to keep still: Stephanos had almost worn a hole in the polished wood floor with his pacing; Georgios must have gone to check that everything was still running smoothly in the counting room at least a dozen times; and Spyros—despite his proclamation of confidence in the passageway last night—seemed to have developed a sudden predilection for hand-wringing. Even *she* didn't seem to be able to stop fiddling with one earring, glancing behind her as the main hall of the mayoral residence filled up with more and more people.

But not Rion. He was perfectly still, hands pressed together, forefingers resting just under his chin. Waiting with the same supreme composure that he'd exhibited from the minute he'd woken up and gone to cast his own vote to the moment he'd returned here to assemble his team for the result. It wasn't the stillness of lethargy— she could see every muscle in his body was pumped with anticipation—instead he seemed to possess the unique ability of being able to keep his body's natural responses under control. A week ago she wouldn't have been particularly surprised about that—nobody got to be the owner of a billion-dollar company without the ability to remain cool at the operative moment—but now that she knew how much this result meant to him personally, she found it incredible.

Almost as incredible as the fact that she would still be here tomorrow, she thought, looking at the dashing figure he cut in his suit, impatient to prove to herself how good the lovemaking would be between them again once the stress of this election was over.

'Ladies and gentlemen.' Georgios's words cut through her errant thoughts and the room fell silent. 'Good evening, and thank you for your patience.' He craned his neck to look at the clock on the right-hand side of the wall behind him, which read just before ten p.m. 'The turnout at the polls this year has been unprecedented, but I can now confirm that all votes have been collected, counted, and verified.' He raised the sealed envelope in his hand. 'People of Metameikos. Your results are in.'

It felt as if the whole room simultaneously stopped breathing and blinking; all energy was focussed on the sound of the envelope being slowly torn open, on the sight of Georgios carefully extracting the slip of paper that held the answer to everyone's future.

He took a deep breath. 'Taking sixty-four per cent of the vote…ladies and gentleman, you have elected a new leader: Orion Delikaris.'

The room erupted in a cheer; Stephanos gave a whoop so loud it was only surpassed by a woman's delighted high-pitched squeal from the back of the room. Libby instantly recognised it as belonging to Eurycleia.

But before the round of applause had reached its natural conclusion there was another loud noise that sounded a lot like a blow being struck. As Libby turned her head, she realised to her astonishment that it had been a blow being struck. Spyros had placed his fist through one of the ornate panels of the eighteenth-century wall.

He swore obscenely, muttered something she couldn't fully discern about a lower class mutiny, then pushed his way through the crowd of smirks and frowns, belatedly followed by his wife, who reluctantly shuffled after him.

But Libby only spared them a single glance, because her eyes were fixed on Rion. She liked to think that if she hadn't already known, then at that moment she would have guessed his motivation for running in this election *was* noble. Because he didn't lord it over Spyros, even though he had every right to do so. His chest wasn't puffed out; he was not self-righteous in his success and newly won power.

No, he looked…supremely humble. Victorious, yes, but as if his victory transcended personal success and belonged to everyone in the room. And, whilst she had seen the tension in every sinew of his body ease slightly as Georgios had read out his name, she also saw a man who was aware that he might have been handed the crown, but it was what he did from this moment onwards which would determine whether he deserved to wear it.

The way all politicians *ought* to look, Libby philoso-
phised, thinking how unfortunate it was that they rarely
did. Yet it made her even prouder to be standing there
beside him.

'Congratulations,' she whispered, squeezing his hand.
'The people of Metameikos made the right choice.'

For a second Rion felt such an acute sense of fulfil-
ment at her words that it even surpassed the moment
Georgios had read out his name. But then he remembered. All she meant was that the other candidate had
been a corrupt pig, and in the absence of anyone else
the people of the old town had been best off choosing
one of their own. Abruptly he let go of her hand.

'I would like to invite the new leader of Metameikos
to the podium, please.' Georgios beamed, gesturing for
Rion to step forward as the disturbance died down. 'A
man who—' he looked at the empty space Spyros had
left behind '—I'm in no doubt whatsoever *is* the best
man for the job.'

Libby felt the uneasiness she'd experienced last night
rise again as Rion dropped her hand without a backward
glance. But as she watched him make his way to the microphone she gave herself a stern talking-to. He was
about to deliver the most important speech of his life, and
all she could worry about was that he hadn't squeezed her
hand and smiled at her in return? Good God! She should
be ashamed of herself. If they were going to build a successful marriage out of the flotsam and jetsam of their old
one, then she really ought to start practising what she
preached: move forward and show him some support.

Her thoughts bore a striking resemblance to the theme of Rion's modest, inspiring and perfectly polished address. He spoke openly about the hard work that lay ahead, without dwelling on what had happened in the past, and shared his vision for the change that was possible, if everyone was willing, for a brighter and more equal future.

As his words turned into actions in the weeks that followed, Libby could well believe he'd been talking about more than just politics. Because after that night things within their marriage undoubtedly changed too. She understood the demands on his time, and why both his work and his political career meant so much to him. In return, to her delight, he began to invite her to accompany him in his duties—to the laying of the first brick for the new hospital, to the occasional meeting with his team. He even asked her to speak at one of them about how she felt the new set of guidelines aimed at restricting planning permission for luxury holiday homes would impact on the tourist industry.

And, though she had expected it to take time for him to fully understand how much having her own life meant to her, he purposely arranged a trip to Delikaris headquarters on the same day that she needed to return to Athens to make some arrangements for the first tour she was due to lead there at the end of the month. He didn't even bat an eyelid when she made a note on the calendar of the dates when she'd be away.

What was more, they made love—often.

Yet, to her distress, even though it seemed that he finally understood the importance of her having her own life, sharing his, the niggling uneasiness remained. In fact, though she'd tried to dismiss it as an old insecurity which would gradually work its way out, like a splinter coming to the body's surface, which only seemed to be getting deeper, causing her to lose more and more sleep.

So much so that one morning, four weeks after the election, Libby sat on the swing seat in front of the fig tree staring back at the house before the sun had even finished rising, and it was Saturday. At least during the week she could pretend to herself that she'd got up early to e-mail Kate before she opened the office for business. But today she had no such excuse.

The truth was that even though the timing finally felt right for them, she still wasn't happy. Because although they made love frequently it had never once been like it was that afternoon. Oh, he had pleasured her body in countless ways, but it always seemed to be about *her* enjoyment, never his. And when she tried to turn the tables—if she sidled down beside him, kissed the hollow by his hipbone and moved to take him in her mouth—he would encourage her away, only reaching what felt like nothing more than a perfunctory climax once she was satisfied.

Maybe it was a superficial reason to be discontent, especially as *he'd* never complained, but Libby had a horrible feeling that it masked something deeper. What if that day in the hallway, when their lovemaking had been so incredible, hadn't been evidence that her defiance had aroused him, but the end of the challenge of seducing her into staying—the age-old thrill of the chase? Then there *wouldn't* have been anything left to excite him the second she'd agreed to stay with him, would there? Just as there hadn't been after their wedding.

And that kind of excitement was never going to last in any marriage unless desire was kept stoked by love.

Libby swallowed down the lump in her throat. Yes, she'd pinned her hopes on that after he'd opened up to her in the walled garden, been convinced it could blossom if only they shared what was in their hearts, but since then they hadn't once talked properly about their relationship. To be perfectly frank, he was more closed off than ever.

Or at least that was how she saw it. But had she bothered to make him understand that and find out how he saw it? No. Libby flexed the soles of her flip-flops, annoyed that she still didn't seem to have learned not to jump to conclusions without consulting him.

Well, that wasn't strictly true. She *knew* she needed to talk to him, she was just afraid. Because what if he turned round and told her she had it spot-on? She couldn't bear it—not now. But the thought of repeating the mistakes of the past was worse. She took a deep breath and stood up.

He was in the kitchen when she came in through the back door. The sight of him wearing nothing but some pale lightweight trousers made her stomach contract.

'Up early again?' he asked, studying her for signs of

nausea. She did look pale. 'Sit down.' He pulled out one of the stools from beneath the breakfast bar. 'Coffee?'

'Umm…yes, thanks.' She wasn't in the least bit thirsty, but it occurred to her that having something to occupy her hands might be a good idea. As he turned to remove a mug from one of the cupboards on the opposite wall, she was grateful that it also gave her the chance to begin without his eyes boring into her. 'Rion, there's something I need to talk to you about.'

Rion stared into the open cupboard. It *had* happened, then. He'd guessed as much from all the early mornings. His heart began to swell with joy, but he forced himself to restrain it. Because, despite his best efforts to make her forget the pedigree he was lacking over the course of the last month, it was obvious from the look she'd worn as she'd walked in the back door that he hadn't succeeded. It was the same look that she'd worn intermittently ever since that night, and he knew this was anything but a joy to her.

'I can guess,' he said grimly, turning back round to face her.

'You can?' Libby blinked up at him, her heart starting to pound.

'It doesn't exactly require a detective, Libby.' He finished pouring the mug of coffee and slid it across the breakfast bar towards her.

So she hadn't imagined it. There *was* a gaping hole in their marriage. She knotted her hands around the mug and raised it to her lips, glad to have the opportunity to at least partially obscure her face for what was coming next.

'Then I need you to tell me how you feel about it.'
Tell me there's a chance there might not be a gaping hole for ever.

'I don't think *my* feelings are the issue, do you?

Libby frowned. 'Of course they are.'

Rion shook his head. No, he knew what this was. She wanted him to come out and say that *he* wasn't a hundred per cent happy about it to stop her feeling guilty because that was how *she* felt. She was out of luck.

'I wanted a child five years ago, Libby. I still do.'

'What?' Libby choked on her coffee.

He did a double-take, suddenly aware that perhaps they'd been talking at cross purposes. 'You *did* want to talk to me about the fact that you're pregnant, didn't you?'

'That I'm…?' She looked at him, aghast, her mind struggling to process what he was saying. 'No, that it isn't… I'm not— Why would you think that?'

His swollen heart shrank and his voice became droll. 'It *is* a frequent outcome when two people have a lot of unprotected sex. Even two people as different as you and I.'

The objects of the room began to blur before her eyes. 'But we haven't been having unprotected sex. I told you, I'm—'

Horror coursed through Libby's veins. That night at the mayoral residence, when she'd said using a condom wasn't necessary, she hadn't actually spelt out why, had she? But surely he couldn't possibly have assumed that without discussion, when their relationship was still so fragile, she'd meant—?

'You're *what*?' he said impatiently.

Yes, she realised suddenly, he could have. Her head began to whirl. He'd spent the last month making love to her as though it was nothing but a functional exercise because that was precisely what it had been. He'd been trying to get her pregnant. And, much as she longed to believe that the reason he wanted that was because he loved her, the look on his face told her it categorically was not. For when had he ever promised any such thing? Never. He'd invited her here to play the role of his wife, and then he'd asked her to stay on. She realised now it was just an extension of their original agreement. Yes, maybe she had convinced him that an independent wife was better than a bland, clichéd one—yes, all his motives were honourable—but at the end of the day what mattered most was his electorate and showing them he was the ultimate family man in the most deliberate way there was.

'I'm on the pill,' she said wretchedly. 'I thought you realised when I said—'

'Of course,' Rion bit out, humiliation washing over him. 'How foolish of me. It should have been obvious that you'd do everything in your power to protect yourself from having my child.'

Libby shook her head. 'I was on the pill anyway. I have been for five years.'

His nostrils flared in disgust. The way she'd expected them to that night, when she'd naïvely taken his lack of reaction as a sign that their marriage was on the mend. She should have realised he hadn't understood what she was saying at all.

'For convenience,' she added. '*Never* for contraception.'

Never? Rion's head shot up. Her eyes met his unhesitantly. Was she saying…? Yes, he realised, she was. Part of him felt infinitely triumphant, yet the other part of him only grew angrier.

'So you've *always* known that no other man could bring you the pleasure that I do?' He slammed the jug of hot coffee down on the breakfast bar. 'Doesn't that tell you that Mother Nature never intended you to give a damn about class?'

Libby frowned. *'Class?'*

Rion exploded at her ingenuous expression. 'For God's sake, Libby! Isn't it about time you stopped pretending? Maybe the thought that you share the same prejudice as your father *does* make you ashamed, but I already know it's why you walked away. I know it's why you fought this for so long, and I know it's why the idea of having my child disgusts you.'

Libby's eyes frantically searched his face. She was hoping she'd misunderstood him. But for the first time in weeks his expression was one of openness and honesty. The kind of expression she'd longed to see but which she'd now do anything to make disappear.

Her mind traced back over the past—how obsessed he'd always been with bettering their situation in Athens, how reluctant he'd always been to discuss his past with her—had it really been because he believed she didn't think he was good enough?

It had been, hadn't it?

Libby's whole body began to shake. She was horrified that he'd spent all those years thinking she was wired that way, that it had never occurred to her that *that* was what was going on in his head, that he'd never told her. That in leaving she must have doubled the insecurities he'd battled with for so long.

'I've never thought that way, Rion. Not the day we met, not the day we married, not ever.'

He looked thoroughly unconvinced. But then she supposed he'd spent most of his life hearing people tell him he was worth nothing, hadn't he? The Spyros family, her father… Well, the latter at least she might be able to go some way to putting right.

'Anyway,' she added, 'if I did share my father's perspective I would have come back years ago.'

His head shot up a second time.

'When my father heard about the success of Delikaris Experiences he tracked me down and called me up, wanting a reconciliation with both of us.' Libby's voice turned sour, but she kept her eyes focussed on his face, not forgetting her purpose in relaying the story. 'When I informed him that we were separated, he promised that if I returned to you he would welcome us back with open arms and make you the heir to Ashworth Motors. When I refused, he swore he'd never speak to me again as long as he lived.'

Rion stared at her in disbelief. Thomas Ashworth had *wanted* her to stay married to him? Had come to consider him a worthy son-in-law regardless of his background because of what he'd achieved? Not long ago that would have felt like the ultimate accomplishment. Now her father's good opinion just felt like an insult. As hollow as defeating Spyros had felt.

Because, no matter how long he'd spent telling himself otherwise, the only person whose good opinion he really cared about was Libby's. He flicked his eyes up to meet hers, guilt forming a lump in his throat. Could it really be possible, then, that he'd had it all along? That he'd been wrong about everything?

'Are you telling me that…you have no objections to having my child?'

Libby looked up at him desperately, feeling the tears prick behind her eyes. If he'd told her that he loved her, that he wanted her to be the mother of his child, nothing would have made her happier. But he hadn't—because he didn't.

'I couldn't bring a child into this world unless he or she would be guaranteed two parents who want to be married to one another for the right reasons.'

Libby watched as Rion closed his eyes. When he opened them again they looked completely changed, as if he'd finally faced that whatever he'd once felt for her had withered away. It had returned briefly, when their relationship had been fresh and exciting again, but now it was gone.

'And that's never going to be us, is it?' he murmured.

Libby felt her heart shrivel and die inside her chest. She'd come inside to talk to him about the gaping hole in their marriage, to find out whether there was any chance he could ever truly love her. She hadn't asked that question but she had the answer, and it was as clear as the result of a landslide election.

'No,' she whispered brokenly, 'it's not.'

And that was why she had to leave.

CHAPTER THIRTEEN

THE muffled slide of a suitcase from beneath a bed, followed by the opening and closing of wardrobe doors, seemed to Rion to be the most depressing sound on earth. He strode to one side of the living room and then back again, afflicted for the first time in his life by an inability to keep still. He wanted to go up there and kiss her until she agreed to stay. But he understood now that that would be as cruel as locking a bird in a cage.

His eyes skimmed the table where she'd been working yesterday, its surface scattered with brochures and scribbled notes. How had he not realised that earlier? If not five years ago, then at least that night at Georgios's, when he'd seen for himself that she needed freedom like other people needed air. But he'd been so blinded by his own inferiority complex that it hadn't occurred to him that when she'd argued that the sensible thing to do was get divorced it had been because she didn't want to be married full-stop.

Now he understood that so long as she remained his wife, no matter how hard he tried to support her career or give her space to spread her wings, she was always going to feel trapped. Not because of his past, but because to her marriage itself was a prison. Or at least marriage to *him* was a prison. For a while there she must have believed there was a chance her feelings could change, that the desire she felt for him might grow into the right reason for wanting to stay, but he knew now there was no way it ever would, and so did she. He'd already done her too much wrong.

But he swore he'd do her no more, no matter how persistent the urge to take the stairs two at a time and haul her back into his arms. What was that phrase? If you loved someone, you should set them free? He raked a hand through his hair, the thought of letting her go excruciating. But, much as he believed in challenging accepted wisdom, he knew he should have heeded that advice a long time ago.

Rion reluctantly walked the short distance to his study and removed the sheaf of papers from the bottom drawer of his desk—the papers he'd placed there after she'd tossed them down the stairs at him, the ones she'd first pulled from her bag that day at his office in Athens. He'd been so determined not to sign them that he'd never read the small print. He didn't read it now. If it asked for anything he'd gladly give it to her, just so he never had to see that look of desolation on her face again. But he knew it didn't ask—knew nothing but walking out of his front door with the signed papers in her hand could ease her expression of torment.

And after that he'd never see her face again, he

thought dismally, glancing round his office at the photos of the latest progress on the hospital, at the plans for the new affordable houses. The things which ought to buoy him up but just left him feeling numb. Because, yes, he'd done everything that he'd sworn he would the day Jason died: made a success of himself, returned to Metameikos and fought for the position which would allow him to make sure nothing like that ever happened again. Only now did he realise that it had been at the expense of his own happiness, that life was only truly worth anything if you had love. Someone to share it with.

But he knew that he had realised it too late. Even if Libby had thought that she wanted to share her life with him once, he could never make her happy now. There was only one thing that could.

Rion looked back down at the papers before him and opened the glass cabinet next to his desk. He poured himself a measure of Scotch, knocked it back, then reached for his pen.

As Libby kneeled on the floor, pressing the mass of unfolded clothes into her suitcase, she could taste the salty drops of her tears. They weren't the hysterical tears of sudden grief, they were the resigned, silent kind, mourning a death that had been inevitable for months—in her case years—but that didn't make them any less painful.

Because all that time, even when she'd told herself not to, she'd kept hoping it wasn't terminal, that underneath it all he *had* wanted her to be his wife, for the same reason that she'd wanted him to be her husband: love.

But now there was no hope left, and she didn't know how to begin to live without it. Even locked in the cupboard under the stairs at Ashworth Manor, she'd had that much. Now all she had was a void in her heart where hope used to be.

'You'd better not go without this.'

She hadn't heard him ascend the stairs or enter the room behind her, but then her mind was such a mess it was a miracle that any of her senses were working at all. Quickly she brushed the tears from her cheeks. But before she could even move on to attempting the neurological function required to process what he'd said, he slid something onto the bed in front of her.

The divorce petition.

The *signed* divorce petition.

Her eyes dropped from the official court logo down to the 'O. Delikaris' scrawled without hesitation on the line. It was the only thing she'd come here originally to get—the thing she'd once imagined would bring with it a sense of closure. She'd never been more wrong about anything in her life. It felt as if she'd been torn open.

'You were right in the first place,' Rion said quietly, unnerved by the way she didn't even move her head, needing to fill the silence because he was afraid that if he didn't the temptation to press his lips to the back of her neck might overwhelm him. 'This is the right thing to do.'

'Thank you,' she choked. It felt as if she were trying to swallow a loaf of bread without chewing.

'I can fly you back to Athens,' he said stiltedly, 'or drive you to the airport if you'd rather?'

The thought of sitting beside him in the plane or next to him in the Bugatti was unbearable. She shook her head and found the courage to turn around, needing him to know she was grateful for the offer.

'If you could just call me a cab, I'll make the arrangements from there.'

Of course, Rion thought helplessly. Anything else would encroach on her independence. He nodded and turned on his heel. 'I'll let you know when it's here.'

The taxi arrived ten minutes later. She'd been watching out of the upstairs window for it to arrive, and was already halfway down the stairs with her suitcase when he called her. She knew it was rude not to have gone and waited with him once she'd finished packing, but she couldn't have trusted herself not to break down, nor have borne him awkwardly trying to comfort her if she had.

'Let me take that,' he insisted, swooping to grasp the handle of her suitcase.

'No, I'm fine, honest—'

He cut her off mid-sentence. 'Please. Allow me that much.'

Libby relinquished her grip, the feel of his hand moving over hers too agonising to even contemplate doing anything else, then followed him downstairs.

'So I guess this is it?' he breathed, placing the suitcase down on the marble.

She nodded, the irony of standing just metres away from the spot where they'd made the most incredible love not lost on her. 'I guess it is.'

The silence was deafening.

Rion fought the urge to offer her money, or the use of his apartment in Athens. 'You'll file the papers when you get back to the city?'

Libby felt her stomach lurch. He seemed so keen to have it all over with now.

She nodded. 'I'm sure the solicitor will send you copies, along with the decree absolute once it's finalised.'

'It should come through pretty quickly, since we're both in agreement.'

His voice seemed to Libby to go up at the end of his sentence, almost as if it was a question. But she told herself not to read anything into it. She'd spent six weeks reading things that weren't really there, that had never been there.

'I should go. The taxi's waiting.' She stepped forward and reclaimed her suitcase. 'I can take it from here.'

With great effort he forced himself to take a step backwards. 'Who knows? Maybe we might bump into each other if you run those excursions here some time.'

'Maybe,' she agreed. Though in her heart she'd already made up her mind to tell Kate there was no way she could carry on with the Greek tours. There was no point in pretending that her memories would do anything other than destroy her if she remained on Greek soil. Maybe even if she didn't.

'Well, in the meantime, I hope your tours in Athens go well.'

She wanted to look back. She wanted to give him a blithe smile and say *Thank you. Good luck running Metameikos too.* She wanted to be glad they understood each other now, if nothing else. But she wasn't, and she couldn't. It took everything she had to place her fingers around the door handle and wrench it open.

'Goodbye, *gineka*—' He stopped himself and sighed deeply. 'Goodbye, Libby.'

'Goodbye, Rion.'

If the sound of Libby packing her things had been the worst noise in the world to Rion, then the click of the door latch as she pulled it shut behind her was Libby's equivalent. Leaving him once had been hard enough—but then she'd been sure their marriage would have broken them both if she'd stayed, had been able to throw herself into discovering who she was and what she wanted. But now that she had, all her discoveries had led her to was the fact that she was completely and irrepressibly in love with him.

She swallowed hard, tears thick in the back of her throat. As much at the discovery that he'd spent all those years believing that in her eyes he'd never been good enough as for the end of their marriage.

But what would he believe now? she wondered. The thought made her whole body jolt forward. *Did* he fully understand that had never been an issue to her? She hadn't actually explained the real reason why she hadn't felt able to agree to have his baby, hadn't told him that a huge part of her wanted to. And, even though she knew it would change nothing, the thought that he might be in any doubt—now or in years to come—that maybe they *still* didn't fully understand one another, clawed at her heart.

She closed her eyes, contemplating whether she could

bear the pain involved in putting that right. She wasn't sure she could, but maybe that was why she *should*. Maybe, in the absence of any other kind of closure, just going back in and saying the words, leaving them there in the hallway, was the closest she was going to get.

'Are you ready to go, Kyria Delikaris?'

Libby's eyes flew open to see the taxi driver, looking at her from his vehicle with a mixture of perplexity and concern, and it suddenly occurred to her that standing outside Rion's front door with tears rolling down her cheeks was an exceptionally thoughtless thing to be doing. Whilst he'd have to publicly confess that they were getting divorced at some point, he didn't need speculation starting now.

'I just—need to do one last thing,' she replied, and without giving a second thought to the pros and cons she turned and rang the doorbell.

Rion opened the door instantly. If she hadn't known better she would have guessed that he'd been leaning up against it, contemplating whether to come after her.

He stared at her, hollow eyes wide. 'You've forgotten something?'

She hesitated for a moment. 'Yes.' She supposed you could put it that way.

Rion did a quick mental tour of the house. 'Of course—your work.' He stepped back, encouraging her to wait inside. 'It's still on the table in the lounge. I'll get it.'

'No—I mean—yes, please—in a minute. But that wasn't what I came back for.'

'Oh?'

'I just…need you to know something.'

He turned fully back to face her, and nodded to confirm that she had his undivided attention. Her misgivings quadrupled, but she forced herself to go on.

'I need you to know that the reason I said I didn't want to have your baby has nothing to do with your past.'

'I know,' he said softly.

Libby knotted her hands together self-consciously. 'Good, I just didn't want you to think—'

'I don't.'

An awkward silence descended.

'I'll get you those papers, then,' he said, disappearing from the hallway.

Libby looked at herself in the mirror on the opposite wall, appalled. *Oh, yes, Libby. Great job of expressing your feelings.*

He returned swiftly, his hands full of her brochures and notes, but she didn't even register them.

'In fact,' she bulldozed on, before she lost her nerve, 'there's no other man I would want to be the father of my children, if I had any. It was one of the reasons I married you then.' *And it's one of the reasons I'd marry you again tomorrow,* she almost said—until she realised how ridiculous that would sound, given that there was a taxi waiting outside to carry her and her suitcase containing their divorce papers away from him for ever.

One of the reasons I married you *then,* Rion noticed. Before she'd realised that marriage and a family couldn't make her happy. He felt a certain relief that it sounded as though she didn't foresee any other man being able to change her mind. Yet the thought that she'd never have any children, his or not, made him infinitely sad. She'd make a wonderful mother.

'You don't have to explain. I know that married life could never make you happy.' His voice grew self-critical. 'It's taken me too long, but I understand now that freedom and independence are the only things which can.'

She did a double-take, her heart beginning to pound in her ears. *That* was the reason why he thought she didn't want his child?

'Then you misunderstand, Rion.' She shook her head, relieved that she *had* turned around on the doorstep to set the record straight. 'Crazy, I know, but the only times in my life when I've felt truly free have been times when I was with you.' Their wedding day. Making love here in the hallway. Inside that lift.

Rion took a step towards her, the tempo of his breathing beginning to accelerate. 'Then why are you leaving?'

She dropped her eyes, tears hovering beneath their lids. 'Because the only times I've ever felt that kind of freedom have been times when I stupidly thought it was possible that you might love me as much as I love you…the way I've loved you ever since I was fifteen years old—so much that when I'm not with you it feels like I'm only half alive.'

'You think I don't love *you* that way?' Rion bit out, trying to stop his own tears from falling, almost unable to believe what he was hearing. But Libby wasn't looking at his face. She was staring at the floor, stifling her own sobs.

'I know you don't. Maybe you had a passing attraction to me once, when I presented you with a challenge, but—'

Rion's foot came into view, and she realised he'd taken another step forward and was now only inches away from her. He placed his forefinger under her chin, tilted her face upwards, and smoothed her hair away from her eyes before she had a chance to even try and hide behind it.

'A *passing attraction*?' he repeated in disbelief. 'You think what I feel for you is a passing attraction? I can't tell you how many times in the years since you left I've wished that was all it was—so I could just forget you, stop wishing you'd come back and move on.' He shook his head. 'I never could. Libby, I want you so much that when I'm with you I can barely control myself—so much that it makes me ashamed.'

'Ashamed?' Her eyes widened. 'Why ashamed?'

'Because you are my wife, and you do not deserve me taking my own pleasure like the boy from the streets that I am.'

Libby's mouth fell open and her heart-rate rocketed. Good God, had what she assumed was uninterest in her in bed really been him thinking he was showing her *respect*? Was it possible that it could always be the way it had been when they'd made love here, in this hallway?

'Rion, I *wanted* to bring you the pleasure you brought me. I didn't want to experience it alone; I wanted to experience it *with* you. I wanted to experience *everything* with you. That's what marriage is about.'

Rion nodded with more than a hint of self-recrimination as he truly understood for the first time the damage he had done to his marriage all those nights he'd worked late, failing to see that she didn't care about money, that she just wanted to be with him.

'It took the thought of you leaving to make me realise that—to realise that you were right about me being obsessed with making it on my own. After Jason—' His voice was thick with emotion. 'After Jason's death I was so determined not to waste one moment of the life he'd been denied—to become a success and to prove men like Spyros wrong, to make sure that I was giving you the life you deserved—that it didn't occur to me that what really matters is sharing life's experiences with someone you love.'

She gave a sad smile and nodded, trying to contain her soaring heart. 'I bet if Jason could tell you what he missed the most it wouldn't be not having all of this, but not being here by your side, to share it with you.'

He managed the smallest of laughs. 'And trying to beat me at it.' The glazed look in his eyes cleared. 'I'm sorry I never let you share my life properly, Libby. I'm sorry I just assumed—so many things. And I wish...' He raised the brochures still clutched in his right hand before dejectedly placing them on the windowsill. 'I wish we could have lived out our dreams together.'

Libby looked up into his liquid brown eyes, and this time she let her heart soar. In doing so, all the wounds which had been inflicted upon it began to heal, as if it had been doused with a miracle cure. Hope returned. No—

more than hope, *faith*. She wasn't entirely sure how it was possible, but she knew it was real. She could feel it.

Slowly she pushed back against the door until the latch clicked behind her. This time the noise had never sounded better. Then she reached down into to the flat front pocket of her suitcase and pulled out the sheaf of divorce papers.

'And I'm sorry that I wasn't ready to share my life either, that I was so preoccupied with myself that I never tried to understand you. But I don't see any reason why we can't start now, do you?' she whispered.

His eyes blazed with delight in exactly the way she'd been hoping, and it was the final confirmation she needed. He hadn't signed the divorce petition because he'd wanted to. He'd signed it because he loved her, because he'd thought it was what *she* wanted. It wasn't. *This* was what she wanted, what she'd always wanted, only it had taken them five years to be ready to open their hearts and cherish it. Frantically, elatedly, she took the divorce petition in her hands and tore it into tiny pieces, flinging them in the air so they rained down on them like confetti. Or snow.

Rion's mouth slid into a wide, wide smile, and he reached his hands around her waist, closing the remaining distance between them.

'Wait!' she cried. 'I have these to go as well.' She reached down into the pocket of her suitcase again and produced a sheet of foiled pills.

Rion looked at her in shock and delight, but then his face grew sombre. 'You know, nothing would please me more than having a child with you, Libby, but...do you mind if we wait just for a little while?

Libby's expression faltered. 'Oh?'

'It's just there are so many things I want us to do together first.'

'Oh!' This time the sound was pure ecstasy on her lips. 'You mean we should research some Delikaris Experiences for two?' Her eyes danced. 'No, Rion, I don't mind at all.'

'You're certain about that?' He furrowed his brow in concern.

She snaked her arms around his neck and whispered in his ear. 'I've never been more certain of anything in my life.'

He drew back, just enough to look her in the eye, his voice deadly serious. 'Then clearly I have a lot of work to do.'

Libby cocked one eyebrow. 'Work?'

'Indeed—because there's one thing you should be more certain of than anything else in your life.' He grinned, catching her wrists and gently pressing her against the wall. 'And that's that this is a whole lot more than a passing attraction. This is love, *gineka mou*. But don't worry. I fully intend to spend the rest of my life convincing you of it.'

And with that he kissed her, with more passion than she'd ever dreamed possible. A passion that matched her own, and that was accompanied by the greatest sense of freedom Libby had ever known. The freedom of loving, and of truly being loved in return.

LARGER-PRINT BOOKS!

HARLEQUIN *Presents*~

PASSION GUARANTEED SEDUCTION

GET 2 FREE LARGER-PRINT NOVELS PLUS 2 FREE GIFTS!

YES! Please send me 2 FREE LARGER-PRINT Harlequin Presents® novels and my 2 FREE gifts (gifts are worth about $10). After receiving them, if I don't wish to receive any more books, I can return the shipping statement marked "cancel". If I don't cancel, I will receive 6 brand-new novels every month and be billed just $4.55 per book in the U.S. or $5.24 per book in Canada. That's a saving of at least 13% off the cover price! It's quite a bargain! Shipping and handling is just 50¢ per book.* I understand that accepting the 2 free books and gifts places me under no obligation to buy anything. I can always return a shipment and cancel at any time. Even if I never buy another book, the two free books and gifts are mine to keep forever.

176/376 HDN E5NG

Name	(PLEASE PRINT)
Address	Apt. #
City	State/Prov.	Zip/Postal Code

Signature (if under 18, a parent or guardian must sign)

Mail to the **Harlequin Reader Service:**
IN U.S.A.: P.O. Box 1867, Buffalo, NY 14240-1867
IN CANADA: P.O. Box 609, Fort Erie, Ontario L2A 5X3

Not valid for current subscribers to Harlequin Presents Larger-Print books.

**Are you a subscriber to Harlequin Presents books
and want to receive the larger-print edition?
Call 1-800-873-8635 today!**

* Terms and prices subject to change without notice. Prices do not include applicable taxes. Sales tax applicable in N.Y. Canadian residents will be charged applicable provincial taxes and GST. Offer not valid in Quebec. This offer is limited to one order per household. All orders subject to approval. Credit or debit balances in a customer's account(s) may be offset by any other outstanding balance owed by or to the customer. Please allow 4 to 6 weeks for delivery. Offer available while quantities last.

Your Privacy: Harlequin Books is committed to protecting your privacy. Our Privacy Policy is available online at www.eHarlequin.com or upon request from the Reader Service. From time to time we make our lists of customers available to reputable third parties who may have a product or service of interest to you. If you would prefer we not share your name and address, please check here. ☐

Help us get it right—We strive for accurate, respectful and relevant communications. To clarify or modify your communication preferences, visit us at www.ReaderService.com/consumerschoice.

HPLP10R

HARLEQUIN®

A *Romance*

FOR EVERY MOOD™

Spotlight on

─ Heart & Home ─

Heartwarming romances
where love can happen
right when you least expect it.

See the next page to enjoy a sneak peek
from Silhouette Special Edition®,
a Heart and Home series.

Introducing McFARLANE'S PERFECT BRIDE
by USA TODAY *bestselling author Christine Rimmer,*
from Silhouette Special Edition®.

Entranced. Captivated. Enchanted.

Connor sat across the table from Tori Jones and couldn't help thinking that those words exactly described what effect the small-town schoolteacher had on him. He might as well stop trying to tell himself he wasn't interested. He was powerfully drawn to her.

Clearly, he should have dated more when he was younger.

There had been a couple of other women since Jennifer had walked out on him. But he had never been entranced. Or captivated. Or enchanted.

Until now.

He wanted her—*her,* Tori Jones, in particular. Not just someone suitably attractive and well-bred, as Jennifer had been. Not just someone sophisticated, sexually exciting and discreet, which pretty much described the two women he'd dated after his marriage crashed and burned.

It came to him that he…he *liked* this woman. And that was new to him. He liked her quick wit, her wisdom and her big heart. He liked the passion in her voice when she talked about things she believed in.

He liked *her.* And suddenly it mattered all out of proportion that she might like him, too.

Was he losing it? He couldn't help but wonder. Was he cracking under the strain—of the soured economy, the McFarlane House setbacks, his divorce, the scary changes in his son? Of the changes he'd decided he needed to make in his life and himself?

Strangely, right then, on his first date with Tori Jones, he didn't care if he just might be going over the edge. He was having a great time—having *fun*, of all things—and he didn't want it to end.

Is Connor finally able to admit his feelings to Tori, and are they reciprocated?
Find out in McFARLANE'S PERFECT BRIDE
by USA TODAY bestselling author Christine Rimmer.
Available July 2010,
only from Silhouette Special Edition®.

Bestselling Harlequin Presents® author

Penny Jordan

brings you an exciting new trilogy...

Needed:
THE WORLD'S MOST
ELIGIBLE
BILLIONAIRES

Three penniless sisters:
how far will they go to save the ones they love?

Lizzie, Charley and Ruby refuse to drown in their debts.
And three of the richest, most ruthless men in the world
are about to enter their lives. Pure, proud but penniless,
how far will these sisters go to save the ones they love?

Look out for

Lizzie's story—**THE WEALTHY GREEK'S**
CONTRACT WIFE, July

Charley's story—**THE ITALIAN DUKE'S**
VIRGIN MISTRESS, August

Ruby's story—**MARRIAGE: TO CLAIM HIS TWINS,**
September

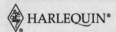

HARLEQUIN®

Showcase

LESLIE KELLY
Naturally Naughty

Wicked & Willing

On sale June 8

Reader favorites from the most talented voices in romance

Save $1.00 on the purchase of 1 or more Harlequin® Showcase books.

SAVE $1.00 on the purchase of 1 or more Harlequin® Showcase books.

Coupon expires November 30, 2010. Redeemable at participating retail outlets.
Limit one coupon per customer. Valid in the U.S.A. and Canada only.

52609057

Canadian Retailers: Harlequin Enterprises Limited will pay the face value of this coupon plus 10.25¢ if submitted by customer for this product only. Any other use constitutes fraud. Coupon is nonassignable. Void if taxed, prohibited or restricted by law. Consumer must pay any government taxes. Void if copied. Nielsen Clearing House ("NCH") customers submit coupons and proof of sales to Harlequin Enterprises Limited, P.O. Box 3000, Saint John, NB E2L 4L3, Canada. Non-NCH retailer—for reimbursement submit coupons and proof of sales directly to Harlequin Enterprises Limited, Retail Marketing Department, 225 Duncan Mill Rd., Don Mills, ON M3B 3K9, Canada.

5 65373 00076 2   (8100)0 11654

U.S. Retailers: Harlequin Enterprises Limited will pay the face value of this coupon plus 8¢ if submitted by customer for this product only. Any other use constitutes fraud. Coupon is nonassignable. Void if taxed, prohibited or restricted by law. Consumer must pay any government taxes. Void if copied. For reimbursement submit coupons and proof of sales directly to Harlequin Enterprises Limited, P.O. Box 880478, El Paso, TX 88588-0478, U.S.A. Cash value 1/100 cents.

HSCCOUP0610